Swinger

Sex

Games

Rachel Richards

Swinger Sex Games

Copyright © 2013 and 2015 Blue Ops and Rachel Richards

Published by Blue Ops 1st Edition October 2013 and includes the following stories: BOP-20, 22, 23, 24, 26, 30, 45, 63, 65 & 67

This Edition: November 2016
ISBN: 978-1-927679-53-1

Contents

Part 1:
Spin the Bottle

Of the four people in the room, two on the couch, two on the loveseat, Mary was the best looking. The thirty-five year old was five-four, one hundred and twenty pounds with large natural breasts, a slim waist and a firm ass. Her long brown wavy hair suited her pretty round face. However, it was her piercing hazel eyes that caught the most attention. When she looked at you, she had you. Or more accurately, you wanted to have her.

"Anyone care for a game?" She asked the other three people in the room.

The couple on the couch looked at her with interest. Karen was a petite blonde with short cropped hair and blue eyes that made her look confident. "What do you have in mind?" She asked.

Mary looked at the only other woman in the room and smiled. Then her eyes shifted to the left to look at Karen's husband, Tim. He was the opposite of her, tall and well-built. His hair was sandy blonde and also very short. He was clean shaven and his rugged look appealed to Mary. "Well?" He asked.

Mary said confidently, "Spin the bottle. My version."

Both Tim and Karen laughed. "God, I haven't played that since high school," Karen said.

"Well?" Frank asked. "Interested?"

Karen looked at Mary's husband and let her eyes study him. She had never been into Italian guys, but to her Frank was cute with his black curly hair and well-toned body. "Sure. Sounds like fun," she said.

Mary cleaned one of the empty beer bottles while Frank got another round for everyone.

"So, how does this work?" Karen asked. "Who goes first?'

"You do," Frank said as he handed her a beer.

Mary placed the bottle on the table. "There are three rounds. The first round is normal. You spin and you have to kiss whoever the bottle is pointing to."

"What are the other rounds?" Tim asked.

"We'll get to that in time," Mary said. Her eyes peered into his, which had an effect on him.

"Okay, what the fuck," Karen said and spun the bottle. It pointed at her husband. "That's easy."

The pair of them embraced and kissed familiar lips. It lasted twenty seconds.

"You're next Tim," Mary said.

"Okay." He spun and to his disappointment, it pointed at Frank.

"Fag," Frank joked.

"Damn."

Frank extended his hand out to be kissed and everyone laughed. Tim couldn't stop laughing as he kissed Frank's hand.

"I'm next," Mary said.

When the bottle stopped, it pointed at Karen. Mary stood up and walked to the center of the room. "Get up," she said to Karen.

Karen rose and the two short women, one thin, one curvy, embraced.

"Are you good with this?" Mary asked to Karen whose face was only inches away.

"Oh yeah. Kiss me already."

Mary leaned forward and Karen met her lips with hers and the kiss was soft and tender. Mary gently slid her tongue between Karen's lips and woke up her tongue. The kiss lasted longer than the thirty seconds, but neither man wanted to stop them.

"That's is so sweet," Frank said.

"Nothing is sweeter," Tim added.

The women broke off the kiss and Mary said to the men. "Shut-up guys." Then she turned to Karen and said, "Thanks."

"You're very welcome. I have forgotten how much I enjoyed kissing girls."

Both women sat down and Frank spun. It pointed at Karen. "Alright."

He stood up and she looked at Tim who told her to, "Go for it."

Frank put his hands on her waist and leaned down to kiss her. She looked up and met his lips. Mary looked at Tim to gage his reaction. To her he seemed to be cool with his wife kissing another man.

Karen broke it off and she sat down beside Tim who told her, "Slut."

She giggled. "Yep. Sometimes."

She spun the bottle and got her husband again. "Damn," she said.

"Damn," Tim said. "So far you are the only one to have kissed everyone in the room."

"Well, I haven't kissed you yet," Frank joked.

"Funny, fag."

Tim was quick to spin the bottle and spun it only enough that it pointed towards Mary. He jumped up quickly. Mary smiled and wrapped her hands around his neck. Their kiss lasted twice as long as the other two smooch.

Mary spun next and got Frank. Then Frank got Tim and had to kiss his hand, Karen got Mary again and for the next two minutes they all kissed their way through the different combinations.

"Okay, Frank get us another round," Mary said. "I think that we need to take a break before we start round two."

Frank left to get the beers and Karen asked," So

how long have you two been in the lifestyle?"

"A couple of years. How about you two?"

"A couple of months. Tonight was only our third time at the club. Before now we've only ever just danced with another couple."

"But we're looking to change that," Tim added.

"I think we just did that with all of that kissing," Karen said.

Frank came back with a round of beers. He looked at Karen and said, "So are you comfortable with what has been going on?"

Karen leaned forward and said, "Yes and I would like to find out what the second round entails."

"A little anxious are we?" Tim joked.

"A little."

So the second round is just like the first, but when the spinner and the spinnie are kissing, the other two kiss as well. So it is a double kiss."

Karen laughed. "Good."

The first spin, Karen picked her husband again and

was getting quite mad at that. The others found it funny. The couples' kissed their own partner for half a minute.

Tim's spin did not please him. It was aimed at Frank. "Not good," he said.

"Good for us," Karen said to Mary.

The two women met in the middle of the room and embraced each other. Their lips met and their husbands enjoyed the show from their seats. Neither one of the men moved from their chairs.

Mary's hand moved from Karen's waist to her nice round ass. She squeezed and enjoyed touching the firm softness. Karen's hands moved up towards Mary big tits and when she got to them she broke of the kiss and looked down at them as she grabbed them with her small hands. They were much bigger than a handful and this act turned everyone on. Karen was excited by playing with large natural breasts, Mary loved being admired and the boys were turned on by watching two hot women being turned on by each other.

Karen kissed Mary again and Mary squeezed her ass bringing her in closer. This pushed Karen's hands into Mary's tits, which pleased both of them.

Mary was starting to think that they might not make it to round three because her and Karen were ready to go to bed now. When she felt Tim press his body against her back she knew that the game was over. She could fell his hard cock pressing against her ass and his hands rubbing against her thighs.

Oh boy, she thought. We will never get past round two.

Then she remembered that the point of the game is to break the ice and get everyone in the mood. It seems to have done the trick. She opened her eyes to see that Frank was behind Karen and was nuzzling her neck.

"Are you good?" Mary asked Karen.

"Yes!"

She looked into the other woman's eyes and asked, "How far do you want to go?"

Karen felt Frank's hands on her ass and she enjoyed being touched by two people at the same time and she wanted more. Much more. "Fuck me," Karen said. "Somebody fuck me."

Mary turned around and said, "Enjoy my

husband."

Karen turned around and both women faced the other woman's husband. This gave the men an invitation. The kissing took on a whole new meaning as before it was only flirting; now it was the start of something serious. The two married couples kissed passionately with Frank's hands on Karen's ass and Tim's hand exploring Mary's over-sized tits.

Mary broke off the kiss and said, "Here, let me make it easier for you."

She pulled off her blouse and Tim's eyes widened as he saw a purple bra struggling to hold two large breasts. Flesh was spilling out over the thin material and Tim was mesmerized by them. Mary put her hand on the back of his head and pushed down. "Enjoy them," she said.

Tim kissed and licked and generally went nuts on the exposed flesh of her tits. Mary unhooked her bra and he pulled it off. They hung heavily and he went, "Oh wow." He took one of her nipples in his mouth and sucked it.

Meanwhile Frank undone Karen's pants and was in the process of sliding them down. Once off he turned around and told her to bend over.

"What a beautiful little arse," he said.

He kissed a cheek through Karen's panties.

Mary playfully pushed Tim away, spun and ran towards the bedroom. Her giant boobs bounced all the way and she had to grab them. At the bed she undid her jeans and took them off. She landed on the bed, rolled onto her back and waited for Tim.

Tim's shirt was off by the time he got to the bedroom. He appeared in the doorway unbuckling his belt.

"Take it all off," Mary said. She spread her legs.

"Fuck. Swinging is fun," Tim said. His eyes were transfixed on the two oversized mounts of flesh.

Still wearing his underwear, he crawled onto the bed and positioned himself between her legs. His cock stretched his underwear and she noticed the bulge. She licked her lips.

Tim lay on top of her and planted her lips onto hers. She wrapped all four of her limbs around him. Her breasts pressed against his hairy chest.

Frank and Karen walked into the bedroom holding

hands. Both of them were naked.

"Is there room for us?" He asked.

Tim rolled himself and Mary over, ending up with her lying on top. His hands grabbed her panties and slid them down.

Karen positioned herself on all fours as Frank went to the night table and got out two condoms. He tossed one that landed on Tim's chest. Mary grabbed it and tore it open.

"A little anxious?" Tim asked.

"Hell yeah."

Since he ate Karen in the living room, Frank knew that she was ready. He slipped his condom covered cock into her as he watched his wife lower herself onto Tim's cock.

The sound of moans filled the room as four people lost themselves in the pleasures of the flesh.

* * * * *

Mary and Frank Salerno liked having sex with other couples when they weren't busy running their cleaning service. Karen and Tim weren't the first the couple that they had swapped with and

Mary hoped that they weren't the last. She loved to fuck. The idea of swinging was her husband's idea and she was slow to get into it. Usually both the other woman and her were reluctant and so things never really progressed that far. She knew what they needed was a good icebreaker and that is why she came up with her version of Spin the Bottle.

The first time they played it was a couple months ago. They had been chatting via messages on a swinger's website for weeks. Pictures were exchanged and they agreed to meet at a local bar at 8 on a Friday.

Mary was, as per usual, nervous and Frank wasn't expecting much. They had met half dozen couples that were attractive, but nothing happened. He figured that all would happen is that they have a few drinks and talk. No sex. He didn't know that his wife had a plan.

Jenny and Karl were both attractive, but gave the appearance that they were a boring couple. And for the majority of their twenty-one year marriage they were; raising three kids while maintaining careers can do that. She was a librarian and he was an accountant and both of them wore glasses. Her hair was thin and straight and she had a curvy figure. She wore tight jeans and a low-cut blouse.

He also had thin brown hair, but looked like he was in pretty good shape.

"I play a lot of basketball," part of their profile on the website said.

Mary preferred guys that were in shape. She didn't really care for muscle bound guys who spent their lives working out in a gym. When she saw Karl and Jenny waiting for them outside of the bar, she was attracted to him immediately.

Because it was a conservative bar, Mary decided not to slut up her appearance too much. She wore jeans and a blouse that wasn't too tight nor showed too much cleavage. Still, her oversized breasts stood out and were hard to miss.

As they approached, Karl and Jenny looked up and smiled. Mary swore she saw Karl glance down at her huge rack and mutter, "Jesus."

Even Jenny could not help but notice. "You match your profile picture," she said. "That's good."

"Why won't we?" Mary asked.

"We find that so many people put up misleading pictures."

Karl laughed. "One couple we met both of them were easily three hundred pounds yet their picture didn't reflect this."

"Why do people do that?" Frank asked. "Don't they know that when they meet the people that you sent the false picture to they might realize that they don't match their picture?"

"Who knows why people do the things that they do." Karl said. "Anyhow, pleased to meet you both. Can we buy you both a drink?"

They found a booth and the conversation and the drinks flowed easily. Work, vacations and hobbies were a few of the conversations that were discussed, all with underlying sexual tension. Mary was well aware that her breasts were on everyone's mind.

After the third round, Karl asked, "Would you both like to come back to our place for the next round?"

Frank didn't have to ask Mary her opinion and said, "We would love to."

* * * * *

The four of them sat uncomfortably on the chesterfield and all of them wanted something to happen.

"Would you like to play a game?" Mary said. She looked around and saw a few nods.

"What is the game?" Jenny asked.

"It is a variation on Spin the Bottle."

"What variation?"

"The first round is normal, but the other rounds are where it gets different."

"How so?"

"You'll see."

Jenny cleaned a bottle and handed it to Mary. "You first."

"No. Your place. You first."

She spun and it pointed halfway between Frank and Karl. "I think that it is Frank," she said.

"Me too," Frank said.

He moved over and they kissed. Mary watched Karl and he wasn't jealous at all. She got the impression that he was focused totally on her tits.

When they broke it off, Jenny said to Mary, "You're next."

"Okay." She spun and it pointed at Karl. She smiled.

He got up and sat down beside Mary. Both Mary and Frank looked at Jenny. "You okay with this?" Mary asked her.

"Of course," she said. "Go for it."

She did and as their lips locked, Karl's left hand cupped Mary's right tit and squeezed. He acted like he was never letting go.

After a minute, Frank and Jenny looked at each other and she said, "They're not stopping. We might as well join them."

"Yep."

He moved over to sit beside her. "Hi," she said.

"Hi," he said back. "How are you?"

"Horny," she said looking into his eyes. And then she licked her lips.

"Perfect."

He leaned in and they kissed.

Meanwhile, Karl was obsessed with Mary's tits and he had both her blouse and bra off, which were now lying on the floor. His hands and lips were touching as much flesh as possible.

She undid her pants and pushed on top of his head. He got the message and moved down, sliding her pants off as he did. She raised her ass of the couch and slid off her panties. She was naked and spread her legs. He spread her lips and inserted his tongue, while staring up at her huge mounds of tits. He had a great view and was happy to please her.

Mary looked over to that her husband was far behind. They were still at the kissing and feeling up stage. She looked down and saw that Karl was under her control. "Yes, right there," she told him. "A little slower…good…good boy."

She leaned back and enjoyed the pleasure. When she opened her eyes, she was surprised to see that both Frank and Jenny were standing naked. They were kissing and she had his cock in her hands. Little slut, she thought.

She was a little jealous and had to remind herself

that if she wanted to fuck cute guys like Karl, she had to let her husband play with other women. The first couple of times had been difficult, but the last few times had been better. Now, she was only partly jealous.

Jenny and Frank walked out of the room and she assumed that they were going to the bedroom. Karl noticed this and implied that they go with them.

"No, fuck me here," she said. She didn't want to see them fucking.

He got a condom out of the pants and put it on. He slid inside of her and she said, "Go boy."

"Your tits are amazing," he said.

She concentrated on how the cock slid against the insides of her pussy. He was rock hard and she had been wet since the first round in the bar.

"Huge," he said. "Huge fucking tits."

She heard moans coming from the bedroom. It was Jenny and she sounded like she was being properly fucked.

Go boy Frank, she thought. Fuck that slut.

She clenched her eyes. Karl's penis was rubbing

her in the right way.

The slut's husband knows what to do with his cock, she thought.

Jenny started to pant and Mary knew that she was in process of having an orgasm. She wanted one too so she started to play with her clit as Karl's cock raced in and out of her. She studied his athletic body and liked what she saw. Her free hand touched the parts of his body that she admired. It roamed from his strong arms to shoulders to his chest.

She moaned. She was close.

"Faster boy," she commanded. "Faster. Faster."

Jenny let out a huge moan and instead of getting jealous; the other woman's orgasm turned her on. She had been pleasured correctly and good for her. Now Mary was even closer now. It was just at the brink.

Karl rode her hard.

She massaged her clit quicker.

She started to moan. It was coming.

"So…close…"

She heard the bed squeak and she knew that Frank was now pumping Jenny hard.

"Lucky…little…slut," she whispered. "So…much…pleasure…"

Karl started to jerk as he came. That did it. Mary arched her back, sticking her tits into the air and her pussy exploded. The condom was soiled from both the inside and outside.

That was the first time that Mary really enjoyed herself while swinging. After that she wasn't jealous of the other woman. The got together with Jenny and Karl a couple more times and they never did get to the second round. It wasn't until Karen and Tim that they did.

She decided that they should get together with Karen and Tim again to try get to the third round.

"Next time we have to advance quicker to get to round three," Mary said.

"Yes, we never seem to get past round two. What is round three anyway?"

"You'll see."

Frank sighed. "You mean that I have to wait until

we seduce another couple before I find out?"

"Yes. Is that so difficult?"

"Is there a round four?"

"There is, but we will never get there. Every time that we get to round one, everyone gets too horny. At least this time we actually made it to round two."

"Yes. we should get Tim and Karen back so that we can play round three."

"Good idea. Why didn't I think of that?"

He rolled his eyes at her sarcasm.

* * * * *

Two weeks later, the four of them sat in the living room in basically the same spots as they did last time. The only difference was that Tim and Karen were in the opposite positions on the couch.

Frank said, "The reason we have invited you two over is to play the round that we never got to play."

"So are we going straight through to round three?" Tim asked.

"We could," Mary said, "But let's have one spin in each of the first two rounds first."

They went through the first couple of rounds quickly and after a good warm-up of kisses, Mary explained the rules of round three. "Now, round three is the same as round one, but when you are picked, the picker removes an article of clothing from you."

"Who chooses?"

"The picker."

"Hot."

Karen spun and the bottle stopped pointing at Mary. "Now do we kiss before or after I take off a piece of your clothing?"

Mary looked confused. "I don't know. We have never made it this far."

"Before," Frank said.

Karen and Mary met in the middle of the living room. Karen studied the large breasted woman and decided to undo her jeans instead of going for her sweater. Mary laughed and watched Karen squat to take her pants off.

She stood up and they embraced. Their lips met. It was an affectionate kiss.

Tim spun next and he also got Mary. "Hmmm...he said as he walked towards her. She stood there in a sweater, pink panties as he dropped to his knees. He gripped both sides of her panties and pulled them down. Her sweater barely covered her ass.

"Pervert," she said to Tim.

"Yep." He kissed her and grabbed her naked ass cheeks with both hands.

Mary spun and got herself. She went to spin again, but Frank said, "Nope. Rules state that you have to take a piece of clothing off."

"But this is my game."

"Not anymore. You created it and we're perfecting it."

"You are just twisting it to your advantage."

"Yep." He laughed.

"How do I kiss myself?"

"Kiss your tits," Tim suggested.

She took off a sock.

"No. No. Both. Socks count only as a half each."

"A lot of new rules all of a sudden." She kissed her own hand. "Next."

Frank spun and Mary was relieved that it didn't land in front of her. Three in a row was enough and all she had on was a sweater and a bra. The only benefit was that she had a couple of good make-out sessions.

The bottle pointed at Karen. Frank lifted her blouse up and off. "Hi," she said just before she got kissed.

Karen spun and got Mary. "Again," Mary cried.

Karen reached under Mary's sweater and unclasped her bra. She helped her get out of it while keeping the sweater on. Mary gave her a long passionate kiss as a thank you.

Tim spun and got Frank. "Awkward," he said.

"You guys have to do it," Mary said. "Rules."

The ladies were laughing as Tim grabbed Frank's shirt and lifted it off. Then he kissed him on the cheek.

"Nope, on the lips," Karen commanded.

It was a quick peck on the lips that neither men were comfortable about.

"That's it," Mary asked. "Disappointed."

Mary spun and got herself. "Fuck!"

"You lose," Frank said. "You're out."

"Out?"

The others laughed as she pulled off the sweater and through it across the room. She leaned back and pulled her right tit up to her mouth. She sucked the nipple.

All three people in the room admired the body of the naked woman in the room and Mary knew that she had everyone's attention so decided that she was going to start with or without everyone else. With her free hand she rubbed her crotch. She let a finger slip in.

Karen knelt in front of her and said, "Let me do that for you."

Mary removed her hand to let the other woman lower her head between her legs. Tim moved over and took over licking her right breast. Frank went for the left one.

As each person was pleasuring her, she said, "If this is losing the game, then I want to lose every time."

Karen's hand reached over and felt Frank's erection through his pants. She unzipped him and he took the cue and took off his pants. Karen slapped his husband's ass and told him, "Take over."

"In a minute." He had his head between her large tits.

She took Frank's cock into her mouth. She grabbed the base of it and sucked.

Mary was disappointed that she lost the other two, but Tim's hand took Karen's place. She enjoyed what he was doing.

Without warning, she was lifted into the air. Tim was carrying her to the bedroom. Frank watched them leave as he enjoyed the wet kisses on his dick from Karen.

Mary was placed on the bed and waited as Tim stripped. "I think that I am about to be fucked," she said.

"You got that right. Get down on all fours."

She obeyed and Tim loved the way that her giant tits hung from her body. He came behind her and inserted his condom covered cock into her. "God you have a nice ass," he said. Then he leaned forward and cupped both of her tits.

Mary had no idea what was going on in the other room, nor did she care. She was being laid by a hot guy who loved her body. She felt very sexy.

Frank placed Karen on the bed to her left and she immediately went for her heavily hanging breasts. She licked a nipple as Frank went down on her.

Mary lowered herself and smothered Karen's face with her boobs. Tim wished that was him instead. Karen couldn't believe how much flesh was pressing against her. Then she realized that she couldn't breathe. Her senses became even more aware and the pleasure that Frank was giving her intensified. Oh my god, she thought. I am going to die. But it feels so fucking good.

She jerked violently as her orgasm took over her body and it was enough to push Mary's tits aside to give her enough breathing room. She gasped for air as she continued to cum. She arched her back and screamed with pleasure.

"Wow," Tim said. "Good job Frank." He patted him on the back.

When Karen recovered, she said, "I couldn't breathe. I thought that I was going to die. I think that I just experienced autoerotic asphyxia."

"Or attempted murder by giant tits," Tim joked.

She was about to say something else, but Frank slipped into her. "Oh god. Fuck me." Another orgasm was building.

"Nice one Mary," Frank said. "You almost killed our guest."

"But what a way to go," Tim added.

"Sorry honey," Mary said. She leaned down and tenderly kissed Karen.

Karen came and as she did, she shouted out, "God I love swinging!"

* * * * *

Four naked sweaty people rested on the bed. All had cum at least once. All were done...for now.

"Great game," Tim said. "I like round three."

"Me too," Frank added. "Is there a round four?"

"Yes," Mary said. "Round four is when you are picked; you have to perform oral sex on the picker."

"Nice." Tim liked that.

"Okay, so next time we start at round three and then move to round four."

"I'm for it."

"Me too." Karen said.

Mary looked at Frank. "Are you in?"

Frank looked at Karen's tight little body. "Of course, but I don't think that I am going to wait." He lowered his head between her legs.

Part 2:
A Paradise

All of Mary's five foot four, one hundred and twenty pound body was lying naked on the bed and she wanted to have some fun. She was on her side and looking at the die that was in her small hand. She tossed back her long brown wavy hair and was in deep thought. Okay, if I roll a one or a two I will swallow Frank's cum. Roll a three or a four and I will let him cum on my breasts. Five or six and he can cum on my face.

She thought about that last one and wasn't sure about allowing that. Being cum on was messy.

"Oh what the hell?" She said. "It is just a game."

Frank came into the room and saw that his wife was naked on the bed and looking good. "Wow," he said as he admired her curves. Her giant tits hung down beautifully. "That is a nice surprise."

"It gets better," she said and then rolled the die. It stopped rolling and she looked at it. "A five."

"What's up?"

"Apparently I have to let you cum on my face."

He smiled and took off his pajamas. "Great." His cock was already half erected.

"Grab the baby oil."

Without hesitation he went into the washroom and came back with a bottle which he handed it to her. She poured it onto the insides of her tits and onto his erection. He got onto the bed and slid his cock between her tits as she pressed them together. She loved the expression of pure pleasure on his face. He was getting off.

Frank's thrusts got faster and faster and Mary loved watching the head of his cock peek out and then disappear between her tits. She noticed that pre-cum had already formed on the tip of his cock and Mary was about to tell him to cum when he let it all fly. Cum flew from his cock and landed on her cheek, chin and mouth. It was a healthy load. She opened her mouth and some of it landed inside.

After he stopped cumming and recovered, he asked, "So what was that all about?

"Are you complaining?"

"Hell no. I just want to know what you are up to."

"I came up with a game that improved on our

version of spin the bottle, not that it needed to be improved upon. That game was designed to get everyone relaxed and turned on so they could all get naked and have a fucking good time. So far that game is batting a thousand. It worked. Anyhow, I am a little bored with spinning bottles so I wrote down the rules for game two: A Paradise. We just played the home version." She showed him the pad and it read: For husband's pleasure:

Roll a one or two and swallow husband's cum.

Roll a three or four and let husband cum on breasts.

Roll a five or six and let husband cum on face.

"I like it," he said. "Is there a female version?"

"Yes." She showed him:

For wife's pleasure:

Roll a one or two and husband licks cum off wife's breasts or face.

Roll a three or four and husband has to give oral after cumming inside wife.

Roll a five or six and husband has to French kiss after cumming in wife's mouth.

"Um…," he said.

"I think that I have to work on it."

"Yep. Let me know when you revise it. I'm going to take a shower."

He left.

The more she thought about it, the more she thought that the wife's pleasure part wasn't really to her benefit so she would have to work on that one. Instead she came up with a game that they could play in a bar together. It was:

Roll a one: flirt with a member of the opposite sex of the spouse's choosing.

Roll a two: flirt with a member of the same sex of the spouse's choosing.

Roll a three: dance with a member of the opposite sex of the spouse's choosing.

Roll a four: dance with a member of the same sex of the spouse's choosing.

Roll a five: kiss a member of the opposite sex of the spouse's choosing.

Roll a six: kiss a member of the same sex of the

spouse's choosing.

Roll a seven: make out with a member of the opposite sex of the spouse's choosing.

Roll an eight: make out with a member of the same sex of the spouse's choosing.

Roll a nine: feel up a member of the opposite sex of the spouse's choosing.

Roll a ten: feel up a member of the same sex of the spouse's choosing.

Roll an eleven: get felt up by a member of the opposite sex of the spouse's choosing.

Roll a twelve: get felt up by a member of the same sex of the spouse's choosing.

She wanted to add: watch spouse have sex with a member of opposite sex of spouse's choosing, watch spouse have sex with a member of the same sex of the spouse's choosing, join spouse having sex with a member of opposite sex of spouse's choosing and join spouse having sex with a member of the same sex of spouses choosing, but then decided to save it for the advanced stage.

She decided that she was going to wow them tonight by wearing something that she would where only to a sex club and not to a normal bar. Her skirt was short and her blouse was tight. When Frank saw her, his mouth opened and closed without him saying a word.

"Too much?" She asked.

"A little."

"Good. Then I am ready."

"Remember that we are going to a vanilla bar. They are not used to the things that happen in swing clubs."

"I know. I should get some attention."

"Ah, yeah. Just keep it in low gear, okay?"

"Maybe." She laughed.

A pair of dice was in Frank's pocket and he wanted to keep them hidden. However, when they arrived at the bar, he could have been waving a stick of dynamite because no one was looking at him. All eyes were on Mary and her generous attributes, which were on display, as they walked up to and sat at the bar.

Mary had the rules in her purse and explained that they would only use one die tonight. She was about to get out the rules when Frank said, "I have them memorized."

"Interesting," she said and smiled. "Ready?"

"Yes."

She rolled a one and he said, "Flirt with a member of the opposite sex of my choosing...hmmm..." he looked around.

"Him."

"Who?"

"The bartender."

"Should be easy."

"You might get some free drinks too," Frank said and then walked to the other end of the bar and sat down beside a bar-fly.

Mary undid another button of her blouse and she put her elbows on the bar. She knew that she was displaying a lot of cleavage and that the bartender had a good view of them. Her piercing eyes were trained on the slightly overweight and bald bartender. Mary found him to be attractive in a blue-collar taking care of business sort of way.

Interesting to Frank is that with a large amount of cleavage on display, every straight male in the bar had automatically zoomed in on them. To the jealousy of the other women in the bar, Mary had been quietly the center of attention since her boobs had arrived. Frank had thought that he heard one guy joke that her tits arrived five minutes before she did.

Despite Mary's Bloody Mary still being half full, the bartender came over anyway and asked Mary, "Are you good?"

"I am, thanks. What's your name?"

"John."

"Hi John. I am Mary."

"I've never seen you here before. Do you live in the area?"

"I do."

"You are married, right?"

"Yes, but sometimes I forget that I am." She giggled and smiled at him.

Frank thought, oh geez that was quick.

John didn't know what to make of that statement and was a little stunned. It wasn't until he heard his name that he was brought back.

After the bartender left to serve another customer, Mary rolled again. It was a four. She held up four fingers to Frank and thought, dance with a member of the same sex of the spouse's choosing.

Mary grabbed her drink and walked to the next room where the dance floor was. Frank broke off his conversation with the barfly and followed her. She placed her glass on a tall table and Frank came behind her.

"Did you like the bartender?" He asked.

"Sure. He was sweet."

"I swear that he came in his pants."

"Frank!" She shook her head.

He laughed.

Frank spotted Mary's next conquest. She was dressed in jeans and a wife beater. Her hair was black and short and she wasn't wearing any make-up.

"Looks like a dyke," she said.

"Should be easy then."

Mary walked onto the empty dance floor, knowing that she was the center of attention. Funny, how the dance floor started to fill up as soon as she got on it. Her eyes stared right at the dyke and within a few minutes, the dyke was dancing in front of her. Mary loved having power over people.

Sex may sell, she thought, but sex also controls.

"What's your name?" The dyke asked.

"Mary."

"I'm Jane."

Jane moved closer and Mary never stepped back until Jane put her hands on Mary's waist. Message sent.

After the dance, Mary said, "Thanks Jane," and then started to move away.

"Can I buy you a drink?" The dyke asked.

"Maybe later." She smiled. "Later."

Back at the table, her next roll was a nine. "Feel up

a member of the opposite sex of the spouse's choosing," Frank whispered to her.

"Oh god. Who?" He glared at her husband.

Frank looked around. "Him."

Frank pointed out a skinny geeky looking guy to which Mary replied, "Really?"

"Yes." He tried not to laugh. "Remember it is just a game."

"Well, back to the dance floor."

Reluctantly, she dirty danced with the guy for a song and then broke it off to go to the washroom.

When she got back to the table, Frank told her, "That wasn't long enough."

She whispered, "Fuck off."

Her next roll was an eleven and she took a drink. She knew exactly who Frank wanted her to be with.

"Well?" Frank asked.

"In a minute. I have a plan."

Five minutes later, the dyke got up from her table

and started to walk to the bathroom. "Be right back." Mary followed the dyke into the washroom. Their eyes met. "It is later."

Jane smiled. "Can I pee first?"

"Can I watch?" She raised an eyebrow.

"Sure."

In a stall, the dyke dropped her pants and underwear and sat on the seat. Mary undid her blouse and bra as Jane peed. "Do you like these?"

The dyke's hands were all over Mary's tits and were soon joined by her mouth and tongue. "Fucking amazing," Jane said.

A hand slid under Mary's skirt and was everywhere. Mary was happy to be touched. Jane pushed her back against the door and slid off Mary's panties. Mary raised a leg and her skirt allowing access to her wet pussy. The dyke inserted a finger that went right to the g-spot as her tongue worked the clit.

"God, I love dykes," Mary moaned. "So good."

Jane inserted a second finger and Mary couldn't believe how good it felt. For the next few minutes she enjoyed Jane's attention and forgot where she was and moaned a little too loudly.

"Shhh," Jane told her.

She didn't listen and came all over the dyke's fingers.

Mary gently pushed Jane away. "Wow that was great."

"I never ate someone while peeing before," she said.

"Well, I will let you finish in peace."

Mary leaned in and gave Jane a kiss. "Thank you."

"No, thank you. You're an amazing beautiful woman."

"Thank you."

Mary opened the door and then adjusted her appearance in the mirror. She heard the toilet flush then left quickly. She walked straight over to Frank. "We should go now," Mary said strongly and continued walking.

Frank learned the blow by blow details as he drove her to the next bar. "I wish that I was there to see it."

"Yes, you could have learned something. That dyke really knew what she was doing."

"Oh, and I don't?"

Mary laughed. "Yes you do, but sometimes when you forget to shave...whiskers, ouch."

"So maybe you should become a dyke then."

"Hell no, I like cock too much. Anyhow, your turn."

In the next bar, Frank rolled a two and says, "I am not comfortable with this. I 'm not into guys."

"Are you homophobic?"

"No, of course not. You know that I'm just not attracted to dudes."

"I know. I was just kidding. We can switch all of your same sex to opposite sex then."

"Thanks."

She looked around and said, "I would say for you to flirt with the waitress, but you already have."

He laughed. "Guilty." He rolled again. It was a

five. "Kiss a member of the opposite sex of the spouse's choosing."

Mary had already spotted who she wanted Frank to kiss. She was a pretty brunette that was with a handsome man. The two of them were at the end of the bar and looked like they were only into each other. She was in tight jeans that barely contained her shapely ass and a t-shirt that outlined the shape of her breasts and showed a hint of nipples. Her brown eyes were soft and friendly.

"She is with someone," Frank said. He looked at the tall guy with short black hair and thought that he was too handsome for her to want to be with anyone else. "It will be tough."

"I don't know about that. I think that I have seen them at the club. They're swingers. Or want-to-be swingers."

He looked at them again. "They do look a little familiar. Are you sure that it was at the club?"

"Yes. About seven months ago." She nodded. "Yes, I am sure of it. They were both there. I don't think that they stayed for very long."

Frank took a drink and put the empty glass on the table. "Well, we will know by how they respond when I hit on her."

"It should be easy. I will distract him for you." Her eyes had already captured his and she knew that she was being lusted over.

Frank sighed. "I think that this game has just taken a different turn."

"Yes. Let's play the couple's version."

"Okay. What is that?"

"You will see." She got up. "Let's introduce ourselves."

He was smiling with his eyes as they approached the table and was ready to hear that anything that Mary had to say. If her boobs could talk, he would have gladly listened to them.

As she got to the table, she asked, "Hello. Do you mind if I ask you a question?"

"Ah sure," he said. The brunette wasn't making eye contact. She looked like she wished that she could hide under the table.

"We've seen you two before somewhere and we can't figure it out."

The guy nodded. "Yes. We were talking about the same thing."

"Well, we should introduce ourselves. This is my wife Mary and I am Frank."

"I'm Jim and this it Tina."

"Good to meet you," Tina said.

"Please have a seat."

Mary sat down beside Jim and Frank beside Tina. This was a subtle gesture of their intentions.

Tina was still a little uncomfortable, but didn't say anything.

"So, where was it?" Mary asked Jim innocently.

Jim nodded and looked at Tina who took a drink. Mary looked right into the other woman's eyes and said, "Oh, you remember don't you?"

Tina nodded. "We were only at that club a few times."

"And what happens there stays there."

With the ice broken, Tina started to relax.

"Yes, we did see you there once," Frank said.

"We are not swingers," Tina said quietly.

"We are not really either," Mary said, "but we do have some fun from time to time."

Tina peered at Mary's outfit. "I can see that. I am not as free as you are. I can't put everything on display like you do."

Mary felt like she was just called a slut, but knew that the woman was right. She is a slut. Still, she didn't like being called one by a total stranger. However, before Mary could respond, Frank said, "So obviously you two are interested in some extra fun or you wouldn't have gone to the club."

"Yes but…" Tina didn't finish.

Mary laughed. "Newbies."

"I guess."

"Will you guys go back to the club?" Mary rested her hand on Jim's leg and started to slowly massage it. She figured that if this couple thought that she was a slut then she might as well have fun by acting like one.

"I hope so," Jim said.

"How about you Tina?" Frank asked.

"Um…sure."

"Do you guys want to play a game?"

"Sure, but I would like to get out of her so we can talk more freely."

Outside, in the parking lot they went got into Frank's BMW. Frank offered to take them home, but they declined. Instead, they sat in the car.

Mary got into the back with Tina and the men were in the front.

"Sorry," Tina said. "I didn't want anyone to over-hear us."

"No problem," Mary said. "So, which one of you brought up the whole swinging thing?"

"That would be me," Jim said.

"Of course. It is always the guy." She looked at Frank. "Men."

"We haven't done anything," Tina said. Mary peered at her. "Well, not that much. We haven't had intercourse with anyone."

"So what have you done?"

"Dancing. Kissing. Some fooling around."

"But you want to do more."

"Yes, but I am not sure we are ready yet or something."

"I understand. Anyhow, do you want to play a game?"

"Sure."

"Frank. Dice."

He handed her the dice and she said to Tina, "It is between you and I and we will do what I roll, okay?"

"Okay, but what?"

"Roll a one and we only talk. Roll a two and we make out. Roll a three: heavy petting. Roll a four: finger or give hand job. Roll a five: give oral. Roll a six: have sex."

"Oh god. Really?"

"Why not? Remember that it is just a game."

Tina laughed. "So you will do to me whatever you roll?"

"Yes. Then you roll."

"Nice," Jim said.

Tina said, "Okay, but not sex. Too soon."

Mary nodded. "Six will be a rollover."

"Okay."

"Shall I roll?"

"Why not?"

Mary rolled a two and before she kissed Tina she asked her, "Have you ever kissed a girl before?"

"Yes."

Mary leaned in and the women's lips touched tenderly. They guys watched silently as the women enjoyed each other's tongues. The kiss didn't last long, but it was good.

"Oh, we want to play too," Jim said.

"Okay," Mary said and handed Tina a die. "Go into the front seat and play the game with Frank. Jim get back here."

Once in the front seat, Tina asked, "Who is first?"

"You," Mary told her.

"Hang on," Frank said as he started the car. "I think that we should go somewhere a little more private if we are going to do this."

Ten minutes later, he pulled in behind a school where it was dark. One of the parking lot lights had gone out, which gave a perfect shadow for them to park in.

Tina rolled a three so Frank leaned over and they kissed awhile before she let her hands roam over his body.

Jim rolled a one. "Really?" He asked. "Just talk. No offense Mary, but I want to do more with you than just talk."

"Patience. And now that we have talked, your turn is done."

Frank rolled a two so he kissed Tina again.

Mary rolled a five and as she unzipped Jim he blurted out, "Paradise!"

She took out his cock and put her lips around him. He was about average size, but since she was so hungry for cock right now, it was huge to her. She sucked and Tina rolled again. It was a four.

"Hand job," Tina said.

She reached in and grabbed his swollen member. "Paradise," Frank said, mimicking Jim's earlier reaction.

After a few minutes, Mary stopped. "Oh by the way, the rollover is no more. The object is to get to a six so we can fuck. So, if someone rolls a six, then we all have to have sex."

Since all four of them were horny, no one objected.

"My turn," Frank said. He rolled and it was a one.

"I think that you just rolled a six," Tina said. She looked at Frank with lust in her eyes.

"Yes, I think that I did."

Jim didn't need any more prompting and Mary leaned back. She spread her legs and Jim put on a condom. Both of them had been ready for a while now.

"Don't be gentle," Mary said. "Get right down to it."

He rammed his cock into her and she moaned.

Meanwhile, Frank was also between a woman's legs. He slid into Tina and she whimpered. "Oh Jim," she said. "Um...sorry, Frank."

He laughed. "That's okay. Call me anything you want to."

Mary felt the car rock and enjoyed being fucked by a hot guy. This game worked well, she thought. What is next?

Jim's pounding intensified and she put any thoughts of a new game out of her mind. There would be time for that later. Now was the time for hard fucking.

She moaned and hung on. It is going to be a long hard ride. Paradise.

Part 3:
Musical Closets

Mary and Frank's house was dark except for a large number of candles placed on the floor throughout the house. They were aligned to illuminate several pathways and to set a mysterious mood. As the lights flickered, the hosts sat with another couple in the living room. Jim and Tina had just been served drinks and all four of them waited for the other couples to arrive. Both women were dressed the same. This was by design. Last week Mary had told Tina and the other three women who were on their way to wear a black mini skirt and a sleeveless black blouse. Of course, Mary with her oversized tits filled her blouse out a lot more than the pretty brunette whose shapely little ass was sitting on the couch.

The men too were in uniform. They were to wear black slacks and a black t-shirt. The idea was for them to appear to look identical in the dim light.

"I feel a little intimidated," Tina said to Mary. "You and Frank are the only couple that we have done anything with."

"Remember that it is just a game," Mary told her.

She took a drink. "I know, but I am still nervous."

"The object of these games is to put everyone into a relax mood and then turn them on."

Tina smiled. "What if I don't like the other guys?"

Mary laughed. "Everyone coming tonight is hot."

"Really?"

"I think so. Trust me. You will want to fuck all of them. Frank here is the ugly one and you have gotten it on with him."

"Hey!" Frank said pretending that he was hurt by her statement.

"Well, if cute Frank is the ugly one then it is going to be a really hot night."

Jim added, "So I take it that you have been with all of the other couples?"

"Yes. I have been with everyone who will be here tonight."

"Wow. Four couples."

"Not at the same time."

"Oh, of course."

"We've been with more," Frank added.

"Frank!" Mary said.

Frank laughed and looked at Tina. "I'm kidding."

"No you're not," Jim said. "I'm jealous."

"I'm still intimidated," Tina said.

"Don't be. It is mostly kissing at first. If it gets to be too much for you then just come back here and have a drink. You don't have to say a word. This is supposed to be fun, not stressful."

"Okay." Tina nodded.

The next couple to arrive was Pete and Laurie. She was wearing the prescribed short black skirt that exposed her long thin legs that supported her thin body. The only other piece of clothing she wore was a small black blouse. As per the plan her bra and panties were left at home. Her sandy blonde hair was shoulder length and she wore a little too much make-up that gave her a bit of a slutty look, which of course fit matched the look of all the other women in the room.

He was also blonde and had – even though he didn't wear make-up – a bit of a sleazy look to him.

He was a womanizer and several months ago Laurie suggested swinging in order to get him to stop fucking around on her. To her knowledge it was working. Now, she knew every woman who he was sticking his long dick into. They squeezed onto the couch beside Tina and Jim. Pete's eyes were transfixed on Mary's tits. He licked his lips.

The last two couples arrived together. The two women were similar in appearance. Both were brunettes with long hair and had good bodies. Cathy was the prettier of the two, but Anna had bigger boobs. Mark was Cathy's husband and he was tall and thin while Anna's husband, Doug, was shorter and more muscular.

After drinks and small talk, Mary got everyone's attention in order to announce the rules of the game. A game which she called, `Musical Closets'. She said, "The first round is where the ladies follow the path laid out by the candles to one of the four closets. Two ladies will be in the walk-in closet in the master bedroom. A man will enter one of the closets, close the door behind him and without any talking, proceed to kiss whoever he finds there. Remember no talking! You shouldn't be able to see who you are with."

"Really?" Tina blurted out loud then felt guilty for

interrupting.

"Ladies make sure that you are in the shadows so you can't be recognized. If you are it would take the fun out of it. The idea is not to know who you are playing with."

"Sounds like fun," Laurie added. "With no talking we have to feel our way to see who we are with."

"Exactly. There is a recording that will play music for five minutes then you will get your next instructions, which are: the men move onto the next closet. There you will repeat. You will kiss whoever you find there. And guess what?"

"No talking?" Jim answered.

This brought more than a few snickers.

"That's right," Frank said. "No talking. Just touch-ing."

Mary continued, "The third round is where it gets even more interesting. The person in the closet has to perform oral sex on whoever walks in."

"How about if it is your own spouse?" Tina asked.

"Doesn't matter. You might not even know it is them."

"Interesting."

"Round four is where the ladies switch closets leaving the boys in the closet." She giggled. "Now don't mess this up because we don't want any boys in the closet together."

"Not going to happen," Frank said.

"You got that right," Jim told him.

"I don't know," Laurie said laughing, "that could be interesting."

"No!" Frank said. "If that happens exit immediately."

"But that means that two women are in a closet together," Mary said. "Nothing wrong with that."

"I would like to see that," Doug said and it was echoed by Mark who added, "Me too."

Mary looked at them and said, "Maybe we should have a round with just the women then?"

"Maybe next time."

"Anyhow, round four is where the men go down on the women."

"For how long?" Tina asked.

"Five minutes. The final round is where the men leave again to find a new closet. Then the fucking begins."

"So how do we know if there is more than one person in a closet?" Mark asked.

"If the door is open, then you can go in. Close it so the others will know that it is occupied."

"Sounds easy enough," Doug said.

Mary got up and said, "Come on girls. Let the games begin."

In the kitchen all five of the women met and Mary pointed to the first closet. Anna followed the path of candles and went into the linen closet, which had the shelves removed so she there was room for her to stand comfortably with just enough room for someone else. As per instructions she left the door open.

Tina was sent into the third bedroom and Cathy was sent into the second. Mary grabbed Laurie's hand and led her to the walk-in-closet. There they were to wait with the door open.

Frank started the CD and music started. It was jazz.

Frank knew that Mary would be in the master bedroom so he went into the linen closet. He bumped into someone as he closed the door behind him. Feeling around in the dark he touched a soft person and drew her to him. Their lips met and he enjoyed kissing whoever it was.

Mark followed the path of candles into the third bedroom and slid the closet door open. Slowly he moved in and found a woman. They kissed before he was able to close the door. Whichever woman it was, she was ready to go, despite her trembling a bit.

Doug went into the second bedroom, saw that the door was open, walked in and closed it behind him. He felt soft hands on him so he turned to find her lips. He had no idea who he was kissing and found that exciting.

Pete followed Jim as they walked through the door of the walk-in-closet and closed it behind them. They softly bumped into two women. While feeling his way, Pete's hands touched one of two massive tits and he knew that he was being groped by Mary. He also felt the hands of another person.

He hoped that it wasn't Jim.

After five minutes, the song ended and Frank's voice on the tape said, "Stop kissing. It is time for the men to move onto the next closet. Remember to leave the door open as you leave."

All five men exited and passed each other in the hallway. No words were exchanged, but a few smiles were. Frank went into the second bedroom. Mark and Doug went into the walk-in-closet where Mary grabbed Mark and Laurie kissed Doug. Pete went in the linen closet where he was practically assaulted. Jim went into the third bedroom where he started to make out with his own wife even though he didn't know it. They kissed each other like they haven't done in years.

The second song ended and Frank's voice said, "Men move to the next closet to receive oral."

They didn't need to be told twice and Frank was one of the quickest to exit. He moved quickly to the third bedroom and as soon as he went in, small hands were undoing his pants. One of the ladies had dropped to her knees and was pulling down his pants and his underwear. Tina opened her mouth and guided his erection into her mouth. Frank moaned softly. Even though the touch was familiar he wasn't sure which lady was sucking him. Every woman here has had his cock in her mouth at some point. Tina was also unsure who the cock belonged to. She liked the texture and size of it. This made her feel like a slut. This turned her on.

I've been a good girl for too long, she thought. I've missed out on a lot of fun.

In the linen closet, Anna had already dropped to her knees before Doug walked in. Both of them strongly suspected that they were with their spouse. However, it didn't matter. It was all good.

Cathy was visited by Jim. Pete wanted to be with Mary so he headed back to the closet, but he was too late, Mark had realized he was with Mary so he went out and turned around to head back in. He knew exactly where he had left her in the dark. Pete settled for Laurie instead.

For the duration of the song, the air was filled with the sounds of women sucking hard and men moaning. Nobody wanted the music to stop. Nobody wanted to hear Frank's voice – including Frank - say, "Stop. Women: as the men are putting their dicks back into their pants move to a new closet to receive oral."

Anna left the linen closet, passed Cathy coming out of the second bedroom and was grabbed by Jim in the closet. She could barely close the door. Cathy found a pair of hands and a tongue, which belonged to Pete, in the walk-in-closet.

Mary let the other two women decide where they were going before she took the remaining closet. Laurie went into the third bedroom. Tina went into the walk-in-closet and was lowered onto her back on the floor. She spread her legs. A face buried itself between her legs and a tongue started touching all of the right spots.

Mary found Doug in the linen closet. Men's tongues worked for five minutes and didn't stop when the music did. Frank's voice said, "Oh come on guys, enough already! Stop! And move onto the fucking stage. A table with condoms is in the hallway. Go now!"

Slowly the five men met at the table.

"Nice message Frank," Jim told him. He was grinning.

He laughed. "Was I wrong?"

"No."

The others laughed along.

Since Frank knew that his wife was no longer in the walk-in-closet, he grabbed a condom and headed into the master bedroom. Doug followed him.

Both Cathy and Tina were still on their backs with their legs spread. Frank slid into Cathy and Doug entered Tina. All four people were relieved to be finally fucking. The first four stages, where the constant switching of partners, succeeded in getting everyone in the mood. Basically the same scenario played out in the bedroom closets. Jim humped Anna in the second bedroom and Mark rubbed his cock between Laurie's pussy lips. Moans grew louder and most people figured out who they were fucking.

Mary was joined by Pete who as soon as he discovered her oversized tits he decided that he was going to fuck her hard. From experience he knew that she liked getting fucked that way. He pinned her against the wall and grabbed a tit in each hand. Then he buried her face between them and kissed and licked as much flesh as he could.

"Are you ever going to fuck me?" Mary said.

"Yes."

He raised and spread her legs. With great satisfaction he rammed his long cock into her. It easily parted her lips and filled her up. She usually preferred thick cocks, but sometimes having a nice long one was good. She certainly liked the way that Pete lusted after her. The man was obsessed with her tits.

All four of Mary's limbs were wrapped around Pete and her tits were crushed against his chest. He humped her with fury. He pulled out, dropped to his knees and ate her until she came. He slid back in and she wrapped her limbs around him.

This has to be the best game yet, she thought as his cock pleasured her.

Somewhere between the next two orgasms that rocked her body, she got an idea for the next game. However, she didn't have time to fully think it out. She was lost in pleasure when she heard Frank's voice announce, "Everyone to the master bedroom for an orgy on the bed!"

Mary was shocked. "When did he decide to do that?"

Pete stopped and pulled out. He picked her up and

carried her out of the closet. He made his way to the master bedroom and placed Mary onto the bed. Several other bodies were already lying on it. Here chaos took over. Mary felt a cock slide into her. It was thicker than Pete's so she knew that it wasn't his. A woman was kissing her and she couldn't count how many hands were on her tits.

Four, no five, she thought.

She moaned.

The lips that she was kissing were replaced by a long thin cock. It was Pete's and she gladly sucked it. A couple were humping wildly beside her and judging by their grunts she knew that it was Frank and Tina.

Good, Tina's into it, she thought.

Pete moved down and pushed the hands away. He pushed Mary's tits together and slid his cock between them. He humped them madly.

As Pete was getting off on her tits, she saw that it was Doug inside of her and that it was Frank and Tina fucking beside her. She heard Laurie cry out, but couldn't see her. She saw Mark's upper body and it looked like he had someone in the missionary position on the floor. Apparently it was Laurie.

At the head of the bed, Cathy and Anna were double teaming Jim. Anna was sitting on his face while Cathy was doing a good impression of a cowgirl.

"Save a horse, ride a cowboy," she sung out.

Pete groaned loudly and his cum hit the insides of the condom. If he wasn't wearing one then Mary would have had a load of cum on her face. She was glad for that. With all of this intense fucking she knew that her hair and make-up was messed up enough. Best not to add to that.

Pete left to clean up in the washroom and Doug leaned in to kiss Mary.

"Hi," she said. "By the way good work in the linen closet."

"Oh, how do you know that it was me?"

"Oh I knew. It was damn good and I know your tongue anywhere."

He smiled and both of his heads swelled. This inspired him to fuck her faster. The creaking bed, creaked louder.

Tina moaned noisily as Frank reached climax. He

jerked a few times then collapsed, rolling off her. The bed stopped rocking as much.

Tina's face appeared over Mary and the pretty woman was smiling. "You were right," Tina said. "This is lots of fun."

Mary smiled as she felt Doug's cock massage the insides of her pussy. Her piercing eyes looked into Tina's eyes and she said, "Kiss me."

Tina leaned in and the women's lips and tongues intertwined.

Meanwhile, Anna came in Jim's face before her and Cathy switched positions. Anna rode him in the reverse cowgirl position and she made eye contact with Doug who was still fucking Mary.

"Come here often?" He asked her.

"As often as possible," she said smiling.

"I see that."

She moaned and Doug enjoyed watching his wife get off. It was overwhelming and he lost his load, much to Mary's disappointment.

After he pulled out, Pete was ready to take his place. For the last few minutes, he had been watching Mary and was now hard again. Mary was surprised to be penetrated by him so soon after his first climax.

Tina broke off her kiss with Mary when she heard her husband groan. "Jim is cumming," she whispered to Mary. "He will sleep now."

"You're welcome to stay over," Mary said between humps. "Take one of the bedrooms."

She saw that her husband was now womanless and falling into a coma. "Thank you. I think that we will." She moved over to him to tell him that they were staying.

Cathy and Anna sat beside Frank and started to talk. It was clear that all three of them were satisfied and were winding down. The only people still fucking besides Pete and Mary were Laurie and Mark on the floor. A groan from Mark a few minutes later indicated that this was also coming to an end.

Mary looked up at Pete and started to fondle her breasts. This inspired Pete to finish.

After everyone had left the master bedroom, Mary

looked at Frank and smiled. He too thought that it was a good night.

"So when did you decide to add in the orgy bit?" She asked him.

"While I was making the CD I thought, what the hell. By this time everyone should be horny as hell and willing to do anything. Did I mess up?"

She nodded. "It was good. Very good. Perfect actually."

"I loved it. I am glad that I added it then."

"Well, it is about time that you added something to the creation of these games."

"So, what is next?"

"I'm not sure, but I am pretty sure that it has to do with blindfolds."

Part 4:
Blindfolds

Since the crowd for the last game was so much fun, a month later, Mary and Frank invited the same group over for the next game. The couples present were Tina and Jim, Pete and Laurie and Cathy and Mark. They were sitting around the living room, sipping wine and waiting for the fifth and final couple to arrive.

"We really enjoyed the last game," Laurie said.

"Where do you come up with this stuff?" Pete asked Mary.

"Yeah," Laurie added. "Very imaginative. Do you read it in a book or what?"

Mary smiled. "It just comes to me. I start thinking about sex and people that I want to fuck and I picture different scenarios."

"As she is masturbating," Frank added.

Mary gave him a look to which he smiled back at her.

"Is that true?" Jim asked.

"Jim!" Tina said.

Frank nodded and Mary blushed.

"Mary touching herself. Now that is a perfect image," Pete said.

The doorbell rang and Frank got up to let Anna and Doug in.

"Well Mary," Laurie said. "I think that you got all the guys in the mood."

"And at least one of the women," Tina added. She winked at Mary.

"Hello all," Doug said as he and Anna came into the room. They sat down.

When Frank came in with a couple of glasses of wine for the new arrivals, Mary got everyone's attention by clapping her hands loudly. "Let's begin." She looked around the room and since there weren't any protests, she stated, "The rules for this one are very simple. It is all about wife tasting. We girls will sit in a chair and the men with blindfolds on will go down on us until we achieve orgasm. Simple."

The other four women and most of the men in the

room seemed to like this.

"And is that it?" Pete asked.

"Do you need more?" Laurie said with a smile on her face.

"No, that is just the first round. There is another round after."

"Why are the women first?" Doug asked. "The women are always first."

"Because it is a lot better for you if we get in the mood," Laurie said.

"Besides," Anna said, "if you guys cum first then you'll just go watch sports."

A few of the guys nodded. "That's true," Jim said.

Frank brought in three wooden chairs and placed them in the middle of the living room. He went back and got two more. All five of them were lined up.

"Now," Mary begun, "this is the best part. Men on your knees before the chairs, pick one, it doesn't matter. And put one of these on." She tossed a blindfold to each one of them.

"Oh what the hell," Mark said. "You only live once."

He was the first to obey and one by one they all got down on their knees. From left to right were Frank, Pete, Mark, Doug and Jim.

Like last time, all five women were dressed more or less the same. Each had on a black mini-skirt and a white blouse. "Wait," Laurie said holding up her hand. "Look at these guys on their knees like that. We should take a picture."

Mary laughed. "Yeah, it is pretty funny."

"Don't you dare," Frank said.

That was echoed by a few others.

"Anyhow, ladies," Mary said, "let's all take a seat."

Laurie sat on the chair in front of Frank, Cathy in front of Pete, Anna in front of Mark, Tina in front of Doug and Mary took a seat in front of Jim.

One by one the men reached out, touched a leg of a woman and then moved closer. By feeling their way they manoeuvred between a woman's legs. Panties were removed and legs were spread. The women tried to be as quiet as possible as the men's tongues touched their pussies. Some fingers were inserted while others went a different route. Pete tried to stick his tongue all the way up Cathy's pussy, but only got a few inches in. The pretty brunette put her hands on top of his head and let out a soft moan.

Handsome Jim was licking up a storm much to Mary's delight. Her eyes were closed and like the others, she moaned softly.

Yep, she thought. This was a good idea. A very good idea.

She clutched her massive tits in her hand and caressed them. They were very sensitive right now. The nipples were poking through the blouse.

Jim continued to work and with one figure gently massaging the opening of her pussy, he concentrated his tongue on her clit. The orgasm crept up on Mary and she accidently smacked Jim on the head.

After she finished cumming, she apologized to him. "Sorry."

He took off his blindfold. "No problem."

One by one all the woman came. Anna was the last

and when Mark took off his blindfold all the others were sitting back on the couches looking at him.

"Oh," he said.

"You lose."

Cathy shook her head and said sarcastically to her husband, "I am so disappointed in you. You have to do better next time."

"I won," Jim said to Mark.

Mark flipped him the bird.

Laurie sighed. "Men. To you everything is a game."

"Yep," Pete said. He smiled.

"Well, you will see in the next round that us girls don't try to be the fastest. It isn't a game to us."

"I don't know about that," Cathy said. "I will make my guy cum the fastest."

"Alright, now for the guy's turn," Doug said with excitement in his voice.

The others agreed and were eager to get going.

Mary stopped that. "Nope, let's change things up."

The guys looked disappointed.

"Guys, you will like this. Don't worry." She turned towards her husband.

Frank took away two chairs.

"I will go first with two others. Now, I need two volunteers." She looked around the room. "Let's make it women only for the first round."

"The women again," Doug said.

"For what?" Cathy asked.

"You will see."

"Oh why not," Anna said. "I'll volunteer." She looked at Cathy and added, "And Cathy will too."

Cathy looked at her friend. "This better be good bitch."

* * * * *

Mary was blindfolded and had her hands behind the chair that she was sitting on in the middle of the living room. Her hands weren't tied, but she pretended that they were. It was part of the fun. Someone was touching her tits and someone else was kissing her. She had no idea who it was. She could tell that the person kissing her was male, but which one of the five men in the room?

She knew that it wasn't her husband. She listed in her head everyone who had been invited and were at the party. There was: Pete and Laurie, Mark and Cathy, Doug and Anna and Jim and Tina; everyone who was at the closet party.

Another person parted her legs and slid their hands up her mini-skirt. It was taken off and a pair of lips kissed the front of her panties. Then those too were taken off. Now she was completely naked. Her top had been taken off as soon as she was blindfolded and sat down.

Her hand was gently pulled to the side where it came into contact with the erected cock of the man she was kissing.

She wasn't the only person who was sitting in a chair blindfolded. Both Cathy and Anna were moaning and Mary could only imagine what was being done to them. Both women elected to be actually tied to the chair. Blindfold and bound wasn't something that Mary wanted, but the other two were getting off on it.

Maybe I should try it sometime, Mary thought.

Her thoughts were interrupted by a soft tongue on her clit. By process of elimination she knew that either Tina or Laurie was down there.

So good, she thought.

Her left nipple was in someone's mouth, her tongue was playing with someone else's tongue and a finger had just entered her pussy. She heard more moans coming from the other women and now she added to them. What a turn-on!

She wasn't surprised that an orgasm came so quickly and since her attackers were still relentlessly pleasuring her, it was followed by another orgasm.

She backed off the kiss to scream, "Jesus fucking Christ!"

Oh, you're faking it dear, Laurie said. She was teasing.

Mary shook her head. The voice was a distance away so it wasn't her between her legs. The soft tongue must belong to Tina. She pictured the pretty brunette with soft friendly brown eyes and a great ass. She had kissed her sweet ass on many occasions.

She pulled off the blindfold to discover that she had been kissing and playing with Mark's cock, and yes, it was Tina who had done a wonderful job of eating her and Doug was still playing with her tits. Both men were opposites. As Mark was tall and thin, Doug was the guy with the muscles.

Mary went over to Cathy's chair and saw that Frank was fucking her and Pete had his cock in her mouth. Two on one, nice, she thought.

Anna had Jim's cock in her and Laurie's tongue in her mouth.

Mary clapped her hands. "Okay, everyone switch now," she said. "Who else wants to be tied up?"

"Who is next?" She asked the other nine people in the room.

"Tina said, "Me."

Laurie put up her hand. "Me too."

Pete said, "I will."

All three of them agreed to be tied up. Mary felt like she was missing something. Next time I will allow myself to be tied up, she decided.

Tina took the chair that Mary was on and the cute

little brunette was fondled by Frank's hand as it tried to find her g-spot. A moan indicated that he had found it.

Anna and Cathy both went for Pete's cock and the pair of them took turns sucking him. There was a smile on his face.

Laurie had Doug and Mark sucking her tits.

Mary sat on the couch and watched what was going on. She was joined by Jim. "Great party!" He said. "Best one yet."

"Thanks."

"What is next?"

She didn't know so she changed the subject. She pointed and asked, "Shouldn't you help out Frank there?"

Jim looked down at Mary's tits and shook his head. "He can handle it by himself."

Mary took a drink from her glass of wine and Jim moved closer.

He said to her, "We are so glad that you got us into this whole swinging thing. We are having a lot of fun."

She smiled at him and saw his boner. "I can see that."

Mary watched Frank ride Tina. She knew that she was one of his favorites and she felt a little jealous. "She is pretty," she said quietly.

"That she is," Jim said, "but so are you..." he reached over and cupped her right breast, "...you have these. Wonderful."

She looked at him. "Thanks, but..."

"You're the hostess with the mostess."

Mary rolled her eyes.

Pete came over and sat down. He was naked and he was still wearing the condom that he had just came in.

Mary asked, "Will you be wearing that all night?" She pointed to the spent condom.

"Ah geez, be right back."

Mary took another drink as she continued to watch what was going on. Frank was still pounding Tina, Laurie was being fucked by Doug and Mark had gone over to watch Anna and Cathy make out and finger each other. He wanted to join in, but they were too into each other to allow him in. He had to resort to jerking himself off as he watched.

Mary was contemplating going over to help him out or joining the girls when Pete came back. Interrupting her thoughts, he asked her, "So, why weren't you tied up? It is fun."

She shrugged.

"Come on," Jim said. "Try it once and if you don't like it…"

"Okay, I will allow myself to be tied up some time," Mary said.

"How about right now?" Pete said. He looked at Jim who nodded.

She didn't have time to process this before Jim and Pete grabbed her and carried her to the bedroom. Along the way, Jim shouted, "Mary's gang bang! Come on everyone."

"This isn't part of the game," Mary said.

"New rules," Jim said. "You have no choice."

"Mob rules," Pete said laughing.

The others followed.

She was placed onto the bed, stripped naked and blindfolded again. Her hands were tied to the bed posts and hands were all over her. Another woman was kissing her and judging by her technique, she was pretty sure that it was Laurie who was kissing her. She squirmed with pleasure.

Someone got between her legs and shoved his cock into her. She thought it was Pete and she was correct. He rode her hard. The idea was for him not to think about delaying the ride. There were four other guys waiting for their turn.

Mary hung onto to him as she was being bounced on the bed. It took about fifty or so hard strokes for him to fill the condom. He groaned as he came.

"A very good short ride," she said.

When he left she started to close her legs, but someone else held them open. Next, another man entered her. He didn't seem to be as tall as the previous man.

This could be Doug, she thought.

He too rode her forcefully and she liked it. She was still the center of attraction. Hands were still touching her and she had a pair of big tits rubbing her face. She thought it was Anna's jugs. Her tongue explored the other woman's nipples.

Someone was massaging the opening of her anus. She wasn't sure if she liked that or not, but with everything else going on, it added to her pleasure. Juices from her very wet pussy trickled down onto the person's finger and her anus. It was an interesting sensation.

Doug lasted longer than Pete and didn't cum until he reached almost a hundred hard strokes. Anna's boobs had been replaced by Tina's pussy and Mary's tongue was licking madly at it.

The third man that entered her was either Mark or Jim. Both men were tall and their dicks reflected that. Whoever's penis it was, it filled her up more than the other two and she wondered how much pleasure a person could take.

Jim rode her slowly at first then he gained speed. He got to his top speed and held it for a while. When he groaned as he shot his load, he knew that it was Jim. She would have thanked him, but she had a pussy grinding her face.

When the fourth dick entered her she knew that there would be a fifth.

This had to be Mark, she thought.

The pussy in her face was replaced with another woman's pussy. Mary didn't know it, but she had been taking on couples. When Pete was riding her, it was Laurie kissing her. When Doug was fucking her, it was Anna's tits in her face. She had been eating Tina while Jim had his big dick inside of her, and they were replaced with Cathy and Mark. She would learn about all of this later and would be very pleased. She was happy not to be the only creative person in the group.

Mark finished, but the face sitter never moved until she had an orgasm.

The fifth she knew wasn't wearing a condom and judging by the size and feel of it, she knew that it was her husband's cock that was inside of her.

"Did you enjoy the gang bang?" He asked.

"Yes. I am sure that you loved watching me."

"I did."

He emptied his load into her.

"She's done. Let's go back to the chairs," Frank said.

"Another great game," Anna said as she and all of

the others piled out of the room.

Mary laid there, naked, blindfolded and still tied to the bed. She felt like a sex object that had just been used by a mob of horny people. Actually, she had just been ganged banged by a mob of horny people and she loved it.

From the living room, she heard Tina ask, "Did anyone untie Mary?"

One of the other women came back into the room, untied her hands.

"Thanks."

"You're welcome," Tina said and then left.

Sounds of pleasure came from the living room. It sounded like Anna was really getting fucked and fucked good.

Mary took off her blindfold and propped herself onto one elbow. She was alone on the bed and her pussy was a little sore. It had seen a lot of action tonight.

Five guys back to back, she thought. That is new for me. And I knew every one of them by their dicks. Oh boy, I am such a slut.

She dropped onto her back and covered her face in shame. A minute later, she removed her hands from her face and stared at the ceiling. "What is next for me and my nymphos?" She wondered out loud.

She smiled and even though she was sexually satisfied, she knew that she would want more in a few minutes. From the other room she heard the sounds of flesh being smacked and wondered what was going on.

Part 5:
Bondage

Even though Mary was sexually satisfied, she wanted more. What had just happened was perfect and fulfilled the game's potential. Being fucked by five men and four women at the same time was a major turn-on. She most always liked being in control, but during the few times that she gave it up, she preferred to be gang-banged in the style that just happened. She knew that at any time she could have put a stop to it. Or Frank could.

She rolled over on the bed and stretched. Her large tits rose up and she saw how sweaty she was.

I should shower, she thought. Maybe even take a bath? And maybe with a couple of the other girls.

She was a little tired and sore so she never moved. Instead she listened to the sounds that were coming from the other room and it sounded like spanking. This did not excite her. She had never been into spanking, S & M or B & D. To her, pain was not sex. However, she wasn't against a good smack on the butt once in a while, even though she pretended that she didn't care for it. She was afraid that if she showed that she liked it, it would lead to something more painful than a light smack on the ass.

She heard a few more smacks and then decided that she should go and investigate what was going on. Still, she never moved. She was too comfortable.

"Mary, come in here," she heard Frank command. "What are you doing, sleeping?"

She sighed. "I'll be right there."

She walked into the living room and saw that all four of the women were down on all fours, naked, blindfolded and had their hands bound. Each one of the ladies was being spanked by their husbands and they all squirmed with each hit. Tina was closest to her and Jim was steadily smacking her ass. The look on Tina's face was of pleasure which Mary couldn't understand and thought, I didn't think that she was into this kind of thing.

Anna was beside Tina and didn't looked too impressed every time Doug hit her, but didn't protest. The reactions from the other two women were somewhere in between. They didn't love or hate it.

Frank was watching from the couch. He was

amused with what was going on. His wife was not. Since no one - that she knew of – was into S & M it all seemed to be a joke. "Who came up with this?" She asked.

Doug said, "The men have taken over Mary. Get down on your knees."

Mary was more than a little reluctant until she saw Frank give her the indication that it was all in good fun.

"Not too hard please," she whispered to Frank as she dropped down onto all fours.

Playfully he said, "Maybe, but only if you are obedient, Mary."

She glared at him and he chuckled. "Relax," he added quietly. "It's me."

He tied her hands together with rope, put the blindfold on her and guided her down onto all fours. With her elbows on the carpet, her shapely ass stuck up in midair and her large tits hung until they rested on the carpet. She felt like a sex slave and that excited her.

The first smack startled her even though it was a light hit.

I am not used to this, she thought. I am not sure if I want to get used to this or at least pretending to.

To her it sounded like some of the other women were enjoying this.

"Suck this baby," Mark said.

She couldn't see Mark as he brushed his cock against his wife's face. Obediently she took it into her mouth.

Another hit and Mary shivered.

Frank asked quietly, "You are not enjoying this are you?"

"Not really."

"Okay, no more spanking."

"The bondage I like."

"Really?"

"Yes. I am starting to get used to having no control. I know that I am going to be pleasured, I just don't know how."

"I want you to suck my cock." He rubbed it against her face and she opened her mouth. It slipped in.

To her surprise, he pulled out and pushed her onto her back. Frank caressed her body with his dick. As he moved his hard cock over her tits he admired her curves. He was never bored of her shapely body.

Doug lined up the chairs in a row and interrupted things by saying, "To the chairs ladies. Now."

With their asses red, they knelt in front of the chairs and the men sat down. The men pulled the women closer until their mouths found their cocks. The attitude of the men was summed up by Doug who said, "Suck it bitch." Anna's mouth engulfed his cock and still it wasn't enough for Doug. He looked over and saw Mary eagerly sucking on Frank's cock, Laurie sucking on Pete's penis, Cathy on Mark's and Tina on Jim's. They are enjoying this too much, he thought and then said, "I have an idea."

"What's that?" Frank asked.

Doug put his lips to his mouth and stated his instructions. "All women stop and remain where you are."

All five women released the cocks from their mouths. He loved this. He was in control." When I tap you on the shoulder you will not make a sound as you get up."

He tapped Tina and helped her get to her feet. He took her to the couch and made her sit. With a hand on each knee he spread her legs apart. "Don't move."

Mary felt a tap on her shoulder and she was led to the couch. "Down on your knees," he said.

She obeyed and was guided forward. "Lick."

Mary's lips found Tina's vagina and this surprised her. However it wasn't unwelcomed by either woman.

Next, as Mary was eating Tina, Cathy was led to the couch and Laurie was positioned between her legs. Anna was still down on all fours in the middle of the room and was the only woman not dyking out. Doug had different plans for her.

Pete moved behind Mary and decided to fuck her doggie style as she ate Tina. To her surprise he rammed his cock into her. Doug did the same thing to Laurie and then commanded the others as he pointed to Anna, "Guys make her air-tight."

With no protest from Anna, they moved closer to

her. Mark lay on his back and Anna was guided on top of him. Jim stood dangling his cock in her face until she took it in her mouth. With lube in his hands Frank put it onto the condom that he was wearing. He watched Anna slowly ride Mark's cock as she sucked on Jim's tool. Her large tits swung as she rocked. She was clearly into this. He put both hands on her ass cheeks and admired the smooth flesh. He had a good view of her anus and her pussy as its lips wrapped around Mark's cock. He put lube on his finger and inserted it into her anus. Anna shook and with still no protest, Frank slid his cock slowly into her tight anus. This got a bigger moan from her. With all three of her orifices plugged, she was now air-tight.

Doug watched as he humped Laurie. His wife was taking it from three guys at the same time and appeared to be loving it. He knew that this had been a fantasy of hers for a long time, but she never had the guts to act on it. Now she had no choice.

The other four women were instructed to switch position and partners. Now Mary was being eaten by Cathy and Laurie by Tina. Pete slid into Tina and Doug into Cathy.

Mary felt like a sex slave and for most of the time didn't know who she was touching or being touched by. She gave up trying to figure out who was who and just enjoyed being pleasured.

She felt a cock brush against her cheek and whoever was eating her stopped. Mary took the penis into her mouth and knew that it was Frank. She was correct in assuming that all of the other husbands were now demanding blow jobs from their wives. Mary sucked and sensed that Frank was ready to cum. He started to cum and then pulled out quickly.

Mary felt something warm and thick land on her face. She hoped that it was Frank's cum. "You bastard," she joked. Some of his load landed in her open mouth, which caused her to groan.

She heard Frank laugh and was relieved that it was him. He pulled off the blindfold and she saw that all of the other women had cum all over their faces and that the guys were all laughing. They loved this.

Mary vowed to get even and she knew exactly how she was going to do it. Quietly she smiled, but underneath the little devil Mary was rubbing her hands and grinning mischievously.

For days afterwards Frank knew that Mary was up to something, but didn't know what. He knew that he would find out in time. When he suggested that he wanted to tie her up, she was too agreeable.

"I'm starting to like it," she told him. Then added "But only with you."

That was the important part. She couldn't do this with anyone who she didn't trust. Certainly not Doug.

As she sprawled naked on the bed, he tied each of her limbs to a bedpost. She was vulnerable and was at the mercy of Frank.

Frank was stiff and couldn't keep his eyes off her voluptuous body. He didn't know where to start.

"Tonight, you are all mine," he said.

She smiled, knowing that he would only spend some time rubbing his dick over her body and then go down on her before penetration.

* * * * *

Frank had forgotten about Mary's plotting until he asked her what she wanted to do on the weekend. "I want to tie you up," she said.

"Um, no," he said definitely.

"Why not? You don't trust me?"

He shivered. The thought of being at the mercy of someone else's wimps didn't make him feel comfortable. "It is not that I don't trust you."

"How about if I tie you up so that you can get out of it when you want to. It will be more of a pretend bondage."

"Um…"

"Come on try it. I was a Girl Scout so I know knots."

He sighed. "Okay, we could try it once."

Frank felt nervous as he lay naked on the bed while Mary tied his left hand to the bedpost. It wasn't tight and he felt like he could get out of it.

"See you can get out of it if you want to," she said. "Just wiggle your hand out of it."

She tied the other one. He pulled on the first one and it tightened. He couldn't get out of it. "You weren't supposed to pull on it." Then he pulled on the other one. It tightened too. "Silly boy, I just told you that you weren't supposed to pull on it at all."

"Mary," he said in a panic. "I can't get out of this." He struggled.

"Calm down. I will let you out in a few minutes, if you are good." She laughed.

He glared at her mischievous smile. "What do you want?"

"First of all, Doug is an asshole and I want him banned from any future games."

"Oh really?"

"I don't like the way that he took over my game and in my own house. I don't trust him. He will do it again. He is gone or no more games."

"Agreed and sure, he is gone. I will miss Anna though."

"Oh, she can still come."

"Oh…"

"I really don't like how things went down last time."

"It was all in good fun."

"Was it? Maybe for you men."

"Oh come on…"

"So do you like being tied up and humiliated?"

"Depends what you have in mind." He smiled at her and glanced down at his penis. It moved and she rolled her eyes.

"Maybe I'll just leave."

She got up and walked to the door.

"Mary! I'm sorry. Come back."

A few minutes later, he heard that someone was at the door, but he couldn't make out who it was. He heard laughter.

Mary walked in with a guy that she had never seen before. He had blonde blown dried hair and was better dressed than most guys. Too well dressed in his opinion and he was not comfortable with this.

"This is Lawrence," Mary said. She turned to walk out. "Have fun you two."

Smiling, Lawrence started to undress.

Frank shouted, "Mary!"

When Lawrence was fully undressed, he walked

over to the bed as Frank was struggling to get free.

"Oh relax honey," Lawrence said. He sounded gay. "You might like it."

"Ahhh!"

Laughing Mary and a blonde woman walked into the room. The blonde undressed and Frank admired her slim yet curvy body. His cock stiffened and she noticed.

Mary said, "This is Larry and Sherri, new friends of mine. Sorry, but we had a little fun at your expense."

Frank seemed relieved, but also exposed.

"Don't worry man. I'm straight," Larry said in a normal voice. "I was just playing the part that Mary asked me to."

"Oh great. I would shake your hand but..." He looked at his tied hands.

Sherri climbed onto the bed and went straight for Frank's cock. Meanwhile Mary allowed Larry to undress her.

Frank was powerless to stop anything and had to endure watching his wife be seduced by another man as he received a blowjob from a good looking woman. Suddenly he didn't mind being tied up. Life is rough, he thought.

Sherri lowered herself onto Frank's cock and rode him. She slapped his chest, but it didn't really hurt him.

"Ouch," he said playfully.

She laughed. "I'm in charge Frankie."

"Don't call me Frankie."

She slapped him again. "I will call you what I want to Frankie. I am in control."

He laughed and enjoyed the sensation of a woman's pussy massaging his cock. The view was also very pleasurable.

She stepped up the pace and Mary came over. She rubbed her large tits into him. He had to endure the soft mounds pressed into his face.

Larry rammed his cock into Mary and Frank could feel each of Larry's thrusts. Larry would ram his cock into Mary who would be pushed forward, which Frank felt as her boobs pressed against him. By the expression on her face, he could see that she was enjoying Larry's body.

He couldn't move and had to take the pleasure at the pace of those who were giving it to him. Sherri was riding him hard and Mary's tits were bouncing off his face. The sensation was over-whelming.

He came and wasn't quiet about it.

"Oh he's done," Sherri said stating the obvious.

She lay down beside Frank. This allowed Mary to bury her head between her legs. Larry reinserted himself into Mary while they both stood at the edge of the bed.

Frank could only watch and listen to the moans of the other three people in the room. After ten minutes or so he felt Sherri reach over and play with his cock. He was getting hard again.

Sherri told Mary to stop and then positioned herself in a sixty-nine with Frank. Her blonde pussy was shoved into his face and he felt her suck on his cock. Sherri stirred to the touch of Frank's tongue as the young woman was getting off. She had a firm grip of his cock with her right hand while her left hand played with his balls.

Oh god, I am liking this, Frank thought as he got hard.

Mary smacked Sherri's ass and almost hit her husband's face. The blonde liked it so Mary did it again. She was squirming so much with each hit that Frank had a hard time connecting his tongue with her pussy. If his hands were free he could hold her ass in place. They weren't so it was a challenge to pleasure her. Once Mary stopped spanking her, Sherri shoved her pussy into his face, almost suffocating him. She wanted to cum and needed his tongue to finish her off. Frank gladly obliged.

As Sherri was cumming Mary was also having a good time. Larry's rhythm was fast and furious. She knew that she was next.

* * * * *

"Next time, I want to be tied up," Sherri said as the four of them were getting dressed. Frank was now free and in a good mood. He nodded, liking the idea.

"It is fun," he said, looked at Mary and added, "With the right people."

"Then I definitely want to be next," Sherri said.

"Um...maybe the time after that," Mary said.

Frank looked at his wife. "What do you have in mind?"

The mischievous smile on the face worried him.

Part 6:
Girl Power:
Mary's Revenge

Mary wasn't angry, but nor was she pleased about how the guys took over last time. She admitted that some of it was fun, but some of it was also degrading so that meant it wasn't as fun as it should have been. She knew that the men could not take over again. After all, these were her games and the other ladies trusted her to keep them within a certain framework. The men, led by Doug, would keep pushing the boundaries to a point where it was no longer fun for the women. It had almost gotten to that point last time.

It was rare for a bunch of women to trust in one of them to lead them so Mary knew that things had come to the breaking point. It was time for her to take the power back and when she contacted the other four ladies during the following week; she put her plan into action. And the plan was simple. It was to boycott the games.

At first the men never suspected anything. It wasn't until the next weekend that Frank assumed that things weren't right with his wife. To probe to see if there was a problem he walked into the kitchen where she was loading the dishwasher and asked, "Have you come up with any new games lately?"

"Nope," she said coldly. She never turned around to look at him.

Now he knew that something was wrong. He sat down on the kitchen chair and stated, "Okay, so what is up?" His eyes went down the back of her body.

There is certainly nothing wrong with her body, he thought.

"Nothing."

"Oh I know you too well. Something is up. What is it?"

"Nothing. As far as the games go, nothing. The games are over."

He half expected this. "Why? Why are the games over?"

"I told the girls that I didn't like how the men took over my game and treated us like sex slaves."

"You didn't have fun?"

She rolled her eyes. "Not really. That type of behavior is degrading to women."

Frank tried to mask his frustration. "We talked at the time and you said that you weren't mad."

"I wasn't, but I wasn't that happy about it either. At the time I thought that Doug was getting a little too rough and after talking with the other girls I know that he was out of control. We are all scared that it will progress into something worse, especially Tina. She was thinking of not coming to the games if Doug comes. So, I decided to end them. No more. The other ladies are in agreement."

Frank took a deep breath and asked, "What can I do to help the situation?"

"Nothing. The games are done."

Frank sensed that Mary was bluffing and/or would come around soon. He was wrong. A month passed and Mary displayed no interest in having sex with anyone but her own husband. That was still good and Frank was starting to think that their swinging days were over. He wasn't too happy about that so he asked her, "So, what can I do to convince you to come up with another game?"

"Isn't our sex life enough?"

Frank cringed at the loaded question. "Mary. You know that I love our sex life." His eyes glanced down at her oversized rack.

"Oh, you really want to play a game?"

"Yeah. We could go back to spin-the-bottle. I have some dice."

"We'll see."

That meant no.

Over the next few weeks, Frank got a hold of the other four guys and found out that they were going through the same withdrawal as he was.

"What is Mary doing?" Jim asked.

"She is up to something," Frank told him. "What, I honestly don't know."

"Well, find out," Doug told him. "She needs to find out who is boss."

She is, Frank thought, but didn't dare admit it to the others. She has the great tits and I am a sucker for them.

Frank took Mary to a romantic dinner to soften her up. After her third glass of wine, he asked her what she was up to.

"It is very simple," Mary stated. "We play by my rules or we don't play at all. I think that we girls have proven that."

"Yes, you have. Point taken. We will not take over again. Promise."

"You really mean that?"

"Yes."

"And to make sure, Doug and Anna won't be invited to the next game. Anna is fine with that. Actually, she has an idea. On the night that we are to have the next game, she will tell him that they weren't invited because he got too aggressive and acted like an asshole."

"Oh boy. He will not like that."

"Anna can't wait to see the look on his face. She told me that for weeks after the last time he was getting out of control and was physically forcing her to do things that she didn't want to do."

"That isn't good. He could be charged."

"Anna claims that it wasn't that bad. No lines were crossed. However, Doug has been dancing on it."

"Not good Doug," Frank said to no one in particular. "Not good at all."

"So no Doug."

"Okay. You're the boss."

"Don't you forget that?"

He nodded.

* * * * *

The next Saturday, Mary and Frank greeted the other three couples, Pete and Laurie, Cathy and Mark and Jim and Tina, as they arrived and after a drink all eight of them went downstairs. In the middle of the rec room was a super king size bed. The fireplace was going and was fairly warm. The lights were off and the only lighting was supplied by the fireplace and a few candles at the other end of the room.

"All men lean against the wall," Mary commanded. They did. "Here are the rules. Now you men can only come onto the bed when you are invited. Anyone that comes on the bed without permission means that the entire game ends for everyone. Got it?"

"Yes," a few of them said.

"Okay ladies, Showtime. Time to dyke out."

After the women had all stripped, Tina climbed onto the bed exposing her small shapely ass for all to see. Mary was the first to smack it. This startled Tina and she looked over her shoulder to give Mary a dirty look, but her gaze was captured by the way Mary's oversized tits hung down. They were like two large boulders. Mary brought them closer and Tina rolled onto her back just in time to receive a lot of female flesh in her face. Tina's pretty face was almost completely covered by Mary's gigantic tits. Tina grabbed them with both hands while her mouth and tongue sucked on a nipple.

Meanwhile Cathy and Laurie lay down beside each other and tenderly made out. They hugged as they kissed. Laurie's hands grabbed Cathy's ass.

"Do a sixty-nine," Pete yelled at his wife.

"Yeah, do it," Mark added.

Both women ignored their husband's commands.

Even if they wanted to perform a sixty-nine on each other, they weren't going to now. That would be given into their husband's demands. Tonight was to counter that.

Instead, Jim was invited by them to the bed. The handsome man was stripped and put onto his back. Laurie eagerly sucked his cock and Cathy made out with him while Mary and Tina grabbed a hand each and from behind the bed they pulled out a rope each. His hands were bound before he even knew it. This was out of the view of the other three men leaning against the wall. The woman had made sure of this by strategically positioning their bodies to block the view. The poor lighting helped.

To keep him quiet, Mary covered his face with her tits. Cathy ran and got Pete and Laurie got Mark. Both were stripped and put onto the bed. Mary and Tina worked quickly and bound them before either one knew what was happening.

By now Frank saw what was happening and tried to resist. It took all four women to get him even close to the bed.

"Frank lie down and take it like a man," Mary commanded.

"Do I have to?"

"Yes if you ever want to get laid again."

He groaned and submitted. He too was tied up.

All four men were flat on their backs with their dicks in various stages of hardness. Mary looked at all four men laying side by side to each other and smiled.

"We should take a picture," Cathy said.

"No!" Pete shouted.

"Never. These things have the way of getting all over the net," Frank said.

"Let's do it."

"No," Mary said. "I have something better."

This worried Frank who said, "Oh shit."

Mary continued, "You are all taking your punishment well. There I hope that you have all learned your lesson. So we will realize that when it comes to sex, we girls are in charge. Do I hear amen?"

A few of them said a reluctant amen.

"Well that was lukewarm," Laurie said.

They tried again, but it wasn't much better.

"Fine," Mary said. "Okay ladies let's leave. Maybe they will change their minds later."

Mary was the second last to leave the room, but stopped at the doors. "I have an idea," she turned to Tina. "Don't you think that it is too warm in here?"

"I think so."

Mary and Tina moved a couple of fans that were in the corner. "Let's see if we can cool them down."

They positioned the fans at each side of the bed and aimed them directly onto the men's junk. They turned them on and left.

"Oh don't leave us," Pete shouted.

When Mary and Tina got upstairs they saw that Laurie and Cathy were on the chesterfield locked in a passionate sixty-nine. Cathy was on top.

"Oh my," Tina said when she saw them.

"Come," Mary said to her and led her by the hand to the bedroom.

At the edge of the bed Mary cupped her hands

against the sides of Tina's pretty face. "You're beautiful," she said as she gazed into Tina's soft brown eyes.

Mary kissed her before she could respond. The kiss was long and very affectionate.

Neither of them consciously remember lying down, but there they were, kissing naked on the bed.

Cries from the living room of someone having an orgasm stopped their kiss.

"Is that Laurie?" Mary asked.

"I think so."

"It's nice not having any boys around."

Tina smiled, "I like being with you."

Mary smiled back and looked directly into the other woman's eyes. "We should get together sometime, just the two of us. Maybe a girl's week-end."

"I would like that."

They could hear the men yell that they were cold and/or bored.

"I guess that we should get back to our pricks."

"Not yet." Tina cupped a tit in her hand and fondled it.

Mary closed her eyes and enjoyed being admired by another woman. She moaned when she felt Tina's tongue on her flesh. It surprised her to feel a finger touch her clit.

"Oh my," she said and spread her legs. "Maybe the pricks can wait."

Tina was intense and Mary was the beneficiary of her busy tongue and finger.

Sounds from the other room told them that Cathy's pussy had just exploded in Laurie's face.

Mary knew that she wasn't too far off herself. Tina's tongue licked all the tits she could get as her finger flicker Mary's clit.

A wave of pleasure went through Mary, forcing her to arch her back and cum. And she wasn't quiet about it.

Downstairs the men heard her and called to be part of it.

The women walked back in laughing. They were

only wearing towels.

"Shrinkage," Laurie said looking at the four flaccid cocks.

"What we need is to find men with bigger dicks," Cathy said.

Mary and Tina turned off the fans and there were a few more comments about cold and shrinkage, which the men didn't really appreciate, but they kept quiet.

"What is next?" Laurie asked.

"Now, we sit on a happy face." She looked at the four naked men and each one smiled at her.

"Who are you going to sit on?" Tina asked her.

"A.B.M.Y."

Everyone looked at her blankly.

"Anyone, but my husband."

"Right," Tina said laughing. "A.B.M.Y."

Dropping her towel she climbed onto the bed and squatted over the closest man's face. It was Mark who got an up close and personal view of Mary's pussy and her gigantic tits as they hung over his face.

"Get to work boy," she commanded.

He parted her lips with his mouth and tongue and Mary moaned. She closed her eyes and enjoyed Mark's tongue as it explored her sensitive areas.

By now the other three ladies had copied Mary, Tina was on Frank, Cathy was on Pete and Laurie was on Jim. Men were busy trying to please the women with their tongues. Since their hands were still tied, it was the only way that they could please the women.

After a few minutes, Mary said, "Okay switch. Everyone move down to the right one."

Mary was now on Frank.

"Just be lucky I don't pee on you," she told him.

"Go for it," Frank said then laughed. "I might like it."

Mary sighed and shook her head. "Men."

Frank got to work and as Mary was enjoying her husband's technique she looked over her shoulder to see that all the men were hard and that all the women were getting off in their own way. Cathy was playing with her good sized tits with her eyes closed and her back was arched as she rode Jim, Laurie was staring right at Mark as she commanded him to lick faster and Tina looked like she was about to cum. Mary watched her rock harder and harder on Pete's cock and heard her breathing get more rapid. Tina was the only one of the four women who hadn't cum yet.

She is about to pop, Mary thought. This thought brought her closer to an orgasm herself. Fuck these games are fun. I've missed them. I've forgotten how much I like fucking a group of people all at the same time.

Frank knew how to please his wife and he used just the right amount of pressure on her clit to bring her to the edge of a climax.

Tina was the first to cum and to Mary's surprise, she was next.

After she made eye contact with Cathy and Laurie she said, "Okay girls, keep moving down the line. We have each four men to fuck before this is all over."

Mary lowered herself onto Pete's cock and it felt

good having another man's cock inside of her. It had been too long. The boycott was almost as hard on her as it was on Frank. She never wanted to do that again.

Laurie was on Frank's cock and Tina and Cathy looked at each other. Neither of them wanted to ride their own husbands.

"Switch?" Laurie asked.

"Sure."

Tina lowered herself onto Mark's cock and Laurie onto Jim's meat.

"Okay faster girls," Mary commanded.

They rode the men like a demon.

Frank said, "Oh it is good to be fucking other people again."

"Amen to that brother," Mark said.

"Too bad that Doug wasn't here," Pete said. He was being sarcastic which the others picked up on and laughed.

"He doesn't know what he is missing," Mark added.

"Yes he does," Mary said. "Anna is telling him right about now what they are missing. And more importantly, she is telling him why he wasn't invited. "

"Oh, I feel sorry for Anna," Jim said. "It wasn't her fault and she has to pay the price."

"She doesn't mind. It was her idea to tell him tonight."

"Expect him to be pounding at the door," Mark said. Mimicking Doug he said, "Let me in. Let me in. I want to fuck too." He laughed.

"Okay people," Frank said. "Less talking and more fucking."

With four women riding high in the saddle all four men had smiles on their faces. Yes, they were tied up and naked beside each other, but four horny women were getting off on their dicks. Life was good.

Pete said, "We've learned our lesson, Mary. From now on you alone are in charge."

Mary would have responded to that statement, but she was busy creaming all over Pete's cock. She was in a good place. Her breasts were large and she was in charge.

Part 7:
Team Pool

From the peculiar expression on her face, Frank could tell that Mary had a new game and he was happy about that. It had been months since she had come up with one. It had been a good break, but he was raring to get back into the swing of things. For the next couple of hours he gave her plenty of chances to reveal her new game, but she didn't. Finally he cornered her in the kitchen and asked her, "So, what is this next game of yours?"

"What game?" She giggled.

"Mary…"

"The rules for the game are simple. There are two. Two people per team and each team member must have – and can only have – one hand on the pool cue while shooting. So it involves teamwork."

"Sounds like fun."

"The object of the game was for the teammates to be close to each other. Real close."

Mary used the kitchen island to simulate a pool table and leaned over it. By using a broom, they quickly worked out an effective way of shooting. She would use her left hand as the bridge while he would provide the thrust.

"Sounds good, the group will be…"

"No! I want newbies."

"Okay. Who then?"

"I've already got two couples lined up and they are coming over on Saturday night."

"Then where are we going? What pool hall do you have in mind? I am not sure how much fooling around a vanilla place will allow."

She looked at him and said, "Our new pool table will be delivered and setup tomorrow."

He was shocked, but very pleased. "Come again?"

"We've been talking about getting one for years and that is all we've been doing is talking so I bought one."

"What size?"

"Full. It will be professionally installed tomorrow. It should be already to go by the time you get home from work."

"So, how much was it?"

"Only a third of the regular price. It is the floor model and I also got a deal. For some reason they really wanted my business."

Frank wondered what she was wearing when she bought it, but decided not to ask. She knows the power of her boobs and the effects they have on men. He also wondered if she slept with someone to get the deal. No, he thought, if that was the case then she would have gotten it for free.

"So, what are you thinking?" She asked.

"Nothing. I don't want to know what you did to get such a great deal."

She giggled. "Oh yes you do."

His mouth dropped open. "Mary…"

"Don't worry, I never touched him. I wouldn't want to. He is not a good looking guy. Let's just say I used his office to change my blouse and he just happened to be in there at the time."

Frank laughed. "You had to change your blouse?"

"Well, I spilled coffee on it."

"And you just happened to have another blouse with you?"

She giggled. "My boobs bought us a pool table and we will have it for our party on Saturday."

Frank now knew why Mary had been cleaning and rearranging the basement all day. "So who are these new people?"

"Remember, Cassandra and Marvin? We met them at the club about six months ago. We danced and that is all. She is a Latino with short cropped black hair, a…"

"Yes, I remember. Very sexy."

"So is he." She raised an eyebrow.

"Of course," he said sarcastically and rolled his eyes. "And couple number two is?"

"Another couple that we met and only danced with. Emma and Fraser."

"Oh yes. She is the fiery redhead from Ireland."

"Yes. That is her."

"How do you find them?"

"I've been exchanging emails with Cassandra and Emma for months now. Both women are ready to swap. Both have come close. They just need the right situation."

He nodded. "Show me where you envision this pool table."

* * * * *

Saturday night, Frank looked at his new pool room. During the week, they took the downstairs' guest room and converted it. They had worked hard and the new table looked great in the room. Inspired, they added a small bar with stools and a black leather chesterfield. Mary added a few touches and the room looked great.

"The room looks so classy that I should be wearing a tux," he said to Mary. She was wearing her special little black dress that hugged her dangerous curves and revealed a lot of cleavage. In fact, most of her tits were exposed. One wrong move and she would pop a nipple or two.

She laughed.

If Frank wasn't interested in sex before, he was now. He suggested a quickie before the guests arrived, but that was turned down.

Both Cassandra and Emma showed up wearing their own version of a little black dress. Cassandra's petite body was in the shortest of all three of dresses and it revealed a lot of leg. So much so that Frank didn't have to lean over very far to see her exposed ass cheeks, and to see that she was wearing a thong.

"Very nice," he mumbled to himself.

Her tits were definitely store bought and her dress revealed a good amount of cleavage.

Emma's body was somewhere between Mary's super curvy body and Cassandra's svelte frame with enhanced boobs. Emma displayed a lot of cleavage and more leg than Mary. Her red hair and creamy skin added to her sexiness. As good as she looked; it was her accent that Frank really liked. The six of them drank in the pool room. Frank was behind the bar and Emma and Fraser sat on the stools. Both were drinking something that Frank had just made for them. Mary was on the chesterfield with Cassandra as Marvin leaned against the pool table, listening to them and trying hard not to stare at Mary's humongous rack. They too had newly made drinks from Frank.

"We left Dublin about two years ago and have

been back only a few times so far," Emma said to Frank.

Frank nodded. He loved her accent and kept asking her questions to hear her speak. "Do you miss the old country?"

On the other side of the room, Mary looked down at Cassandra's cleavage and stated, "I take it that Marvin likes his tits big."

Cassandra glanced over at Marvin and caught him looking at Mary's tits. "Is there any doubt?"

Mary smiled at him. He was tall with an athletic body. His hair was short and brown and even though he said that he had a German and French background Mary thought that there was a hint of Latino in his mix. Sexy, she thought.

She looked over at Fraser. He was stockier and not as conservative looking as Marvin. Fraser looked like he could be in a rock band or some other kind of artsy thing. His straight thin hair was almost down to his shoulders and he had a beard. It was very well trimmed and it looked good. Normally Mary didn't go for facial hair, but there was something about Fraser that turned Mary on. She looked at Marvin and also wanted him between her legs.

"I think that we should begin the game," she said. She looked at Frank who was busy listening to Emma. She said louder, "Hello, everyone! Let me explain the rules. Two players per team. Each player must have – and can only have – one hand on the pool cue while shooting. So it involves team-work and you have to work it out between your-selves."

"Okay, sounds interesting," Emma said.

"The teams are Emma and Frank, Cassandra and Fraser and Marvin and I."

"Who breaks?" Cassandra asked.

"Well, its Frank's table," Marvin said. "He breaks."

Emma walked to the table and picked up a pool cue. "How do we do this?" Emma asked Frank.

He stood behind her. "You hold the cue steady with your hand...um, have you played pool be-fore?"

"Yes."

"You know how to make a bridge?"

"Like this?"

"Yes. I will put this there…" he lowered the end of the cue onto her fingers, "…and I will provide the power." He got behind her and softly pressed his crotch into her nice round butt. His free hand held her waist as he pulled his right hand back and pushed it through Emma's bridge towards the cue ball. Once hit, the cue ball slammed into the pile of balls and sent them flying over the table.

"Oh good one went in," Emma said. "Do we go again?"

"Yes."

"Which ball are we going after?"

He pointed to one and she leaned over the table and put her hand onto the table providing a sliding point for the stick. Frank came behind her and placed his crotch against her butt. She could feel that his cock was getting hard and giggled. He placed the stick in her bridge and lined up the shot. His cock was also lining things up. It grew as it rubbed between her ass cheeks.

"Oh my," she said.

He pulled back on the cue and shot. The cue ball hit the other ball on the nose and that wasn't what Frank had in mind. The ball bounced off the side and didn't go into the pocket.

"Oh we missed," she said.

"Next," Mary said and looked at Cassandra and Fraser.

"Okay so I know how this goes," Cassandra said laughing. "I bend over and put my hands on the table and you put the stick into the bridge that I have made with my hand."

Fraser liked the view of Cassandra's curves bend over the table. He did what Frank did and pressed his crotch into her ass cheeks and slid the stick through her hand.

They missed so it was Mary and Marvin's turn. She bent over just like the other women had done, but the difference was that her tits hung all the way down to the table's surface.

"Jesus," Marvin said as he put the stick in her hand. As he stared at her tits, he slid it back and forth and picked up speed.

"I know what you are thinking," Mary said to everyone's amusement and added to his embarrassment, "by the way that is a very nice boner you have." She moved her ass slowly back and forth against it.

"That is not helping, Mary," Frank said.

"On the contrary," Mary said. "His stick is getting bigger and bigger."

Frank moved behind Emma who was standing by the bar. His cock rubbed against her ass cheeks and grew. His hands wrapped around and caressed her thighs.

"Oh my," she said softly.

Fraser and Cassandra were on the couch and he saw that Marvin was stuck. "Are you ever going to shoot boy?"

"Yeah." He pulled back and the balls didn't go where he wanted them to. They missed too.

Frank announced, "I think that we all have to practice. Everyone grab a ball and take a few practice shots."

Emma got into the position and Frank pressed his body against hers. Her hands were on the table and he put the stick in her hand. Slowly he pulled it back and forth as his free hand roamed over her body. She moaned softly and closed her eyes.

Meanwhile Cassandra was in a similar position beside Emma and had Fraser behind her. At least he pretended to line up the balls. At the end of the table Marvin put the cue on the table so that he could touch Mary with both hands. Mary's hands were on the table and her eyes watched the others as she got felt up. From the look on both of the other women's faces; they wanted their brains fucked out. They were ready. Emma turned her head and met Frank's lips.

Okay, one couple is making out, she thought.

A few seconds later, Emma's dress was lifted up to reveal her flawless bum. Mary was a little jealous of her cute little ass. Frank wasted no time. He pulled her panties off, spread her legs and used his tongue to explore her ass and pussy.

She looked at the other couple. Cassandra managed to turn to her side in order to kiss the stud behind her better.

That's two, Mary thought. What a great icebreaker. Time to fuck.

She turned her head to look at Marvin. Her eyes said, kiss me and he wasted no time.

Soft moans were heard and the sexual tension that

had been present since the first guests had arrived was now thick. Six horny people were burning with lust and thinking of nothing else. Mary knew that she was dripping wet. Fucking new people always did that to her. Without warning she was rolled onto her back and the straps of her dress were pulled off her shoulders. Marvin attacked her tits like a starving new born. She placed her hands on his head.

Meanwhile, Emma was approaching orgasm as Frank was now directly underneath her to give himself total access to her pussy. Cassandra was also being eaten, but she was flat on her back with her butt on the edge of the pool table. Her dress was also hiked up. Fraser's head was buried between her legs.

"I want to be eaten too," Mary said.

"What?"

"All of the other girls are being eaten."

Marvin looked over and saw that his wife was getting off. "Does that bother you?" Mary whispered into his ear.

He looked at Mary's huge rack. "No." He parted her legs and pulled off her panties. "Beautiful," he said.

Mary moaned when she felt his soft tongue make contact with her swollen wet pussy lips. She smiled because she knew that she was headed for a nice orgasm.

Frank went behind the bar and pulled out a glass bowl. It was full of condoms. He took one and placed the bowl on the table between the other two couples. "Help yourself boys," he said, but neither one of them could hear. Both of their heads were buried between the legs of a woman who was experiencing an orgasm and weren't quiet about it.

To Frank's surprise Emma had moved to the couch. She was naked and in the missionary position. Frank stripped and put on a condom.

"Are you good with this?" He asked her.

"Shut up and fuck me Frank," she said.

He entered her just as Mary hit the peak of her climax. Listening to her almost made him cum. He rode the busty redhead harder than normal. It had been awhile since he and Mary had swung. He was really turned on. Well, not as much as Mary who was now experiencing another orgasm.

"Jesus. Back to back orgasms," he muttered.

Most guys have stage fright during their first time swapping and Fraser was having his problems. Earlier Frank had pulled the guys off to the side and told them, "Whatever you do, don't think about not getting it up, it only makes it worse. Too much pressure. Instead, just concentrate on the beautiful woman that is naked before you. Admire her features."

Mary had anticipated this from Marvin and had dropped to her knees after her second orgasm. Her cock sucking skills were having a good effect on Marvin. He was rock hard in minutes.

My wife the champion cock sucker, Frank thought. I am so proud.

"Fuck," he said.

"Sure," Mary said. She reached into the bowl, grabbed a condom and slipped it onto his cock. She sat on the edge of the table with her legs spread and fondled her tits. Staring right at them he rammed his cock into her.

Fraser was having his problems too so Cassandra decided to try what Mary had done.

"Fraser doesn't your wife look great with my dick inside her?" Frank said to him.

He looked over and saw the busty redhead flat on her back with all four of her limbs wrapped around Frank. She looked like she was having fun. He was a little jealous and nodded. "She looks awesome."

"Look at my wife."

He saw Mary's chest rise and fall. Two massive melons moved to Marvin's rhythm as she panted.

"That's a lot of tit," he mumbled.

Cassandra was now sucking on a hard cock. It had worked. "You're ready," she told him. "Fuck me." She grabbed a condom and wrapped his Willie.

She too got her ass on the edge of the pool table.

He slid in and blurted out loud," This is a fucking good party."

As people laughed Mary smiled and thought, what a cheesy newbie line.

A couple of good hard strokes later, she had to agreed and said, "Yes, this is a fucking good party."

Marvin came first and collapsed onto Mary. His face was buried in her plenteous mounds. Mary caressed the back of his head. "Good job," she said, "good job."

Frank decided to let it fly and came inside of the cute redhead's pussy. He gently pulled out and sat on the couch. "Thank you," he said to her.

She turned around and laid down resting her head on his thigh. Both of them watched the only remaining couple.

"It is the energizer bunny over there," Frank joked. "Go Fraser go."

"Shut-up guys," he said as he was cumming but nobody could understand what he was saying.

"More drinks?" Frank asked.

After everyone had left Mary took a bath. Halfway through, Frank came in and sat on the edge of the tub. She was leaning back with her eyes closed and he wasn't sure if she knew if he had come in or not. "Congratulations on another successful game," he said.

She opened her eyes, looked at him and said, "Thank you." She closed her eyes again.

"What is next?"

"You are going to join me in here and then you are going to fuck me."

He smiled. "Okay, but I meant what is the next game."

She looked into her husband's eyes and stated, "I have no idea."

Part 8:
Black Friday

Mary wanted something different and decided that instead of shopping she decided to have her own version of Black Friday. At dinner on Wednesday she told her idea to her husband, "We girls will screw an African American guy to see who has the longest dick."

"I don't see the game part," Frank said. He wasn't too impressed because there wasn't anything about what he was supposed to do. Where was his action?

"It is a game and we will get together on Saturday and declare the winner."

"The winner?"

"The woman who had the longest dick inside of her on Friday wins." She smiled at him like it was the most wonderful idea in the world.

He didn't return her smile. "How will you know who had the longest dick inside of her?"

"Simply we take a pic of it with a ruler."

"Okay, but what happens if the guy doesn't allow you to take a picture of it?"

She laughed. "Simple. We will tell them, no pic, no dick inside of me."

"Well…" Frank shrugged. "So you all have to find a guy who will allow you to take a picture of his dick."

"Yes. It shouldn't be a problem finding a man to have sex with us and if the guy is proud of what he has he will only too happy to have a picture taken of it, especially if I make a big fuss of it."

He knew that it was true and rolled his eyes. "So what does the winner get besides a big black dick inside of her?"

"She takes control over the next group activity. She will be Queen for a night. That means whatever she says, happens. If she says that she wants two guys to go down on her, then two guys will go down on her. Simple."

"I can see how you would like that."

"Of course. So do you understand now?"

Frank said, "Yes, but I am a little confused. So what

is in it for us guys?"

"Um…" It was clear that she hadn't thought of that. "…maybe we can have a similar contest to find the biggest booty or something."

Frank groaned. "Wrong. Try again."

"Um…"

"I can see smoke," Frank joked.

"I'll think of something, okay," she looked sheepishly at her husband.

"So this is what your girls' night is all about then?"

"Yes," she hung her head.

"Were you going to tell me?"

"Yes."

"Before or after?"

"During."

"What?"

"The husbands are supposed to be there."

"To do what, hold the ruler against the guy's

dick?"

"No. Take the picture."

"Really? Um, no. Not going to do it."

"No, we want you there...well, for protection. It has been years, no a decade since I've had a one night stand and things are getting scarier out there these days."

"So, what I am supposed to do while you fuck Mr. big dick?"

"I don't know, jerk off."

"Mary!"

"I'll suck you off right after...or during...or something."

He shook his head. "The word cuckold comes to mind." He wasn't amused.

* * * * *

As unexcited about Mary's latest game, Frank accompanied his wife on Black Friday. He wasn't thrilled that the ladies were shopping for long black dick. Mary dressed like a total slut and Frank told her that. She wore black hot pants, a very tight white blouse with no bra. On her feet were a pair of long black boots and she put on more make-up than she usually did.

"I am a total slut. That's why you love me."

All ten of them gathered around a table near the dance floor of a club. The women checked out all of the African American men in the place and the more they looked the more men appeared. They could sense that the women craved dark meet tonight.

Laurie was the first to be picked up and after a couple of dances she and her husband Pete left with a tall handsome African American man.

"Oh damn," Mary said. "I think that he was really hung and that Laurie is going to win."

"How can you tell?" Frank asked.

"He is tall and very confident."

"Afraid to lose?" Frank asked mockingly.

She gave him a look and then checked out what the other women were doing. Anna and Cathy were on the dance floor with a couple of guys and Tina was still sitting at the table with her husband. Mary didn't want to be the last to be picked up so she stepped up her game.

"No," she mumbled and then added, "No...no... no."

Frank watched her cross man after man off her list and then realized that she had selected one. She made eyes contact with a tall handsome man who got the message and came right over and asked, "Care to dance beautiful?"

"Sure."

Mary stood up and felt short next to the man. She was only five foot four and he was clearly over six feet tall. He looked down and saw down her top. "Beautiful," he said. "Come." He held out her hand.

She looked back at Frank as they walked towards the dance floor. The song was a typical dance song which Mary didn't recognize, but it had the familiar beat that most dance songs seemed to use. It pulsed through the speakers. She danced with the stranger and was quickly interrupted. Anna leaned over and shouted in her ear. "We're leaving. Talk to you tomorrow." She smiled. "Good game."

"Remember to email your pic as soon as possible."

"Of course." She waved goodbye.

Mary watched Anna and Doug leave with her choice of African American man and thought a few catty thoughts about her choice. However she was interrupted by the man she was dancing with. He asked her, "Your husband doesn't mind?"

"He likes to watch."

"Dancing?"

"Um, no..." she smiled at him. "...yes, he likes dancing, but he really likes to watch...um, you know."

"Oh..." He took that as a cue to step closer. She smiled at him and he put his hands on her waist. She liked being touched and looked back at the table where her husband and the other guys were watching.

Frank was a little turned on by how sexy Mary looked as she allowed the guy's hands to fondle her ass. Her hands also were roaming over his body. She looked like she wanted to be taken right there on the dance floor. She came in here looking like a slut, he thought. Now she is acting like one. My wife is a total slut.

He sighed and shook his head at himself. He was hard and couldn't believe that he actually looked forward to watching his wife get her brains fucked out. Mary waved at him and he waved back, which the man saw. He should his head and asked Mary, "Can I ask you a question?"

"Sure. My name is Mary."

"I'm James."

"Hi James. What is your question?"

"Does size matter to you?" James' hands squeezed her shapely ass.

She smiled. "Of course. The bigger the better." Her hand ran over his strong chest.

"Cool."

"Can I ask you three questions?"

"Three? Sure."

"Yes the first one will determine the next two questions so be careful how you answer it."

"Okay, I'll think about my answer."

"How hung are you?"

He smiled. "Touch me to find out."

Mary's hand travelled down his torso until it got to his pants. Then with a smile on her face she stroked the front of James' pants. She smiled. She was impressed. It wasn't the longest that she had ever felt, but he was hung. "Very nice." She didn't stop touching it. "I love big cocks."

"So beautiful what is the next question?"

She felt his cock pulse. It clearly liked the attention it was getting. "Oh, so big. Can I take a picture of it…you know for my personal use only? Don't worry I won't Facebook it or anything."

"Um, sure. Not here."

"Of course. We have a hotel a room."

He nodded. "Nice."

"That leads to my next question."

James knew what was coming, but asked anyway, "What is it?"

She looked up into her eyes, smiled and asked, "Can my husband watch us?"

He leaned down and kissed her.

Frank saw them kiss and was oddly turned on by it. "My wife is a super slut," he said to the other guys at the table. I can't believe we agreed to this. What were we thinking?"

"We are guys," Mark said. "We are a sucker for sex. The women can do what they want to."

Mary and James held hands as they walked off the dance floor. They passed the table where only a few of the guys remained. "Goodnight everyone," Mary said.

* * * * *

Frank sat on a chair facing the bed of the hotel room. The lights were low and he could clearly see James sitting on the bed giving him a funny look.

"You good with this?" James asked Frank.

"Sure, we're swingers and this is just one more of my wife's sex games."

"Oh man I'm not sure if I could watch my lady."

Frank nodded. "Just be gentle with her, okay?"

"You got it man." He held out his hand to give Frank a fist pump.

Frank felt a little silly doing a fist pump with a man who was about to fuck his wife in front of him.

Mary came out of the washroom with a smile on her face. "Well now," she said. "It is good to see that you two are getting alone."

She stopped in front of James and held up a foot long ruler.

"You're going to need a bigger ruler than that," James said.

"Really?" Frank blurted out loud.

"No, I wish."

Mary and James kissed and their hands were everywhere and clothes were taken off. James' pants dropped to the floor and Mary dropped to her knees. There was quite the bulge in his underwear. She kissed it and it jumped. She pulled down his underwear and saw a thick cock. She touched it and it got fully erect. She placed the ruler against his cock and mumbled, "Only eight inches, but two inches thick."

She knew that he probably wasn't long enough for her to win. Still, she had a nice big cock staring her in her face and that was a good thing. After she took a couple of pictures she took it into her mouth and she heard Frank say, "Condoms."

"Oh right."

She got up and walked over to her purse. James followed her and grabbed her from behind. His hands cupped her large tits as he pressed his cock into her backside. He slipped his hands into her panties to play with her clit. She moaned and pulled down her panties.

James half dragged her to the bed and put his head between her legs. He went wild and Mary loved what his tongue was doing on her pussy. She came quickly and James wasted no time in sliding into her.

Frank watched James hump his wife. He had a good rhythm going and he knew that Mary liked it. She looked over with a look of total lust on her face. She put her hand to her mouth to indicate to Frank that she wanted his cock in her mouth. He wasted no time getting naked and came onto the bed. He knelt before her.

"Oh man," James said, "you have an awesome wife."

"That I do."

Frank compared dicks. He watched James' cock slide in and out of his wife and tried to gage the size. To him he was a little longer than James, but James was a little thicker.

Mary smiled at him. "Sword fight in my mouth," she said. "James come here."

Mary had trouble getting both men's cocks in her mouth at the same time, but had fun doing so. Both cocks were thick and hard, but one was white and one was black.

This is different she thought. Fucking hot.

With both hands she reached under each man and gently played with their balls.

"Oh god Frank, your wife is fucking hot," James practically shouted. He reached down and grabbed one of her large tits. "And god damn beautiful." He moaned. "God, I can't take it." His eyes roamed over Mary's body and saw that Frank was fingering her. Mary's hips rocked with his touch.

"Let it fly James," Frank said and pulled out.

Mary concentrated on James' cock while Frank slid into his wife. He fucked her hard and she sucked as hard as she could. All three of them moaned.

"Damn!" James shouted as he jerked. He came hard and released quite the load into the condom. Mary felt it and stopped.

James sat back and watched Frank ride Mary. "You two are a fun couple," he said.

Mary wrapped all four of her limbs around her husband and passionately kissed him. James watched them as he dressed. They were still fucking when James was fully dressed and he didn't know what to do. Never having been in this situation before he didn't know what the cool thing to do so he just stood there watching. Frank looked over and said, "I'll be done in a minute, but if you want to leave then leave your number."

Mary smiled at him so James leaned over and gave her a kiss. "Thanks beautiful. That was awesome."

"Enter your number into my phone and hand it to me please," Mary said.

He did and handed it to her while Frank humped her.

"Thanks stud."

"Later guys." James said. "Out of here."

After James left, Frank said, "That was fun. I wouldn't want to do it all the time, but I could do it again sometime."

Mary smiled and then looked at her phone.

Frank was a little amused that Mary was checking her email while they were still fucking. "Are you going to win?"

"I don't know. I don't think so."

"Does that worry you?"

"Yes. I have to win."

"Why?" He increased his speed.

"You'll see tomorrow."

"Sure." He increased his speed even more.

"Oh shit," she blurted out loud. "Damn that Laurie." She held the phone so Frank could see. The photo on the screen showed a foot long ruler against a cock that was almost as long. "She is the winner so far."

"So it isn't you then?"

"No."

"And you don't like that?"

"No."

"So the ten of us are going to have sex and you're not happy because you are not in control of it, right?"

She looked into his eyes and said, "Anyone, but Laurie. God knows what she will get us to do."

Frank laughed and said, "Now, that sounds like it is going to be a party."

Mary glared at him. "Are you ever going to cum?"

He laughed. "Someday."

"Frank."

"Okay, you asked for it." He pulled out and fired his load at her face. The first shot hit her in the left tit and then the next one hit her forehead. The rest of his load landed on her chin and neck.

"Nice," she said sarcastically. "I suppose that I deserved that."

"What, total sluts don't like being covered in cum?"

"I guess that I deserved that too."

"Yep, you do." He laughed. "Good game."

Part 9:
Sexual Roulette

"So what is your next game?" Frank asked Mary. They were driving home from an evening at his parent's house. It was a nice evening, but he could tell that his wife was a little bored with the vanilla evening and had something on her mind.

"Just a game with you and me in the club," she said dispassionately.

"Oh," Frank didn't have to ask why she didn't want to include anyone from the group. Mary didn't like the last game where she wasn't elected Queen because the woman who was elected Queen for the evening saw to it that Mary didn't get any attention from anyone until the very end. Waiting wasn't fun for her and when she finally got fucked, it was humiliating. Everyone but her husband thought that it was funny, but it was easily the worse night that she has ever had since she had joined the lifestyle. She vowed to get even and knew what her revenge was. She was going to fuck them over by not fucking them.

Mary said with a little more energy, "So the game is - and you will like this part because it could involve only women - sexual roulette."

"Nice." All he could think of was images of putting a gun to his head and they were replaced with women.

"Well, you're not bi so the game doesn't work if we both don't play with men. Since we both like women, it works with these rules." she smiled.

"I am liking this. You me and other women."

"Well, there might be a guy or two."

Frank looked confused.

"You will see."

* * * * *

Mary was dressed in a skimpy black dress that showed plenty of cleavage and the sex club was busy. They found a table that had a view of the dance floor which was filled with couples and a number of single women.

Frank asked Mary when and how the game would begin.

Mary said, "So we pick six singles and assign them all a number. We each roll a die and whatever comes up is the person we have to seduce."

"What happens if we both roll the same number?"

"A three-way. We fuck the number together."

"And if we fail to seduce her?"

Mary gave him a look. "You lose and you have to wait until the other person is done."

"If we both strike out?"

"We start again with new numbers."

"Okay let's pick the six women," Frank said while looking at the women on the dance floor.

Mary gave him a look and shook her head.

"What?" He said. He was confused.

"Only five will be women. One number will be a man."

"Oh shit. What happens if I pick his number?"

"Seduce him or lose the round." She laughed. "And if you lose two rounds you are out. Also the second round will have two guys and four women."

Frank shook his head.

Mary scanned around the club and then said. "There is number one." She pointed to a tall thin blonde with long straight hair and was in a skimpy black dress that was similar to what Mary was wearing. The only difference was that Mary had a lot more curves than the other woman. Still, the slim woman looked good. "Agreed?" Mary said.

"Hell yes," Frank said. "And number two should be her friend."

"Her?" Mary looked at the brunette and said, "No. I know her. She is a major fucking bitch."

Frank didn't bother to ask why she hated that woman. He really didn't want to know and allowed Mary to pick the rest of the list.

Number two was a little suicide blonde in a flowered dress, number three was a busty brunette in a low cut blouse and tight jeans, number four was a petite redhead with short cropped hair and number five was a dark skinned woman in a white dress. The guy was number six and he was a handsome stud in jeans and a button-down shirt. All appeared to be single and unattached at the moment.

"Ladies first," Frank said.

Mary rolled a four and Frank rolled a six. "Shit!" He said.

"Have fun," Mary said to him and then kissed him on the cheek. "I won't be long."

Mary walked onto the dance floor close to where the petite redhead was dancing with a couple of friends. Mary smiled at her and was immediately invited into the group of dancing women.

Frank watched from the sidelines as his wife danced closer and closer to the sexy little redhead. This turned him on.

The redhead smiled at Mary. "What is your name?" The woman asked.

"Mary. What is yours?"

"Rachel. You have great tits." The redhead stared at them and licked her lips.

"Thank you. You can touch them if you want to."

Rachel didn't waste any time and her small hands reached up and cupped Mary's big tits. "Wow."

Mary leaned in to kiss her. Rachel accepted and Frank got an erection watching two hot women make-out on the dance floor.

Rachel continued to grope Mary's tits after they stopped making out. "Your great tits are making me so wet," Rachel said.

"I make you wet?" Mary asked, pretending to be surprised.

"Yes," she said nodding. "Very wet. You are so beautiful. I want to fuck you."

"Then let's go to the play area," Mary said.

Frank watched his wife and the redhead walk pass him. He couldn't believe how quickly Mary had seduced another woman. When she puts her mind to things, he thought. She either gets what she wants or she moves on.

Mary allowed the redhead to push her onto the bed and lift her dress. Rachel went straight for Mary's tits. She groped them, licked her nipples and generally had a great time with the large breasts.

"I love women with big tits," Rachel said passionately. It was clear that she was getting off on Mary's attributes.

Opposites attract, Mary thought as she studied the petite woman's body. She is tiny and has small boobs so naturally she likes the opposite of her body type.

Mary closed her eyes and enjoyed the attention. Having someone lose themselves in passion was great for her fragile self-esteem. She liked being lusted over by both men and women.

"Go down on me," Mary said.

Rachel moved down Mary's curvy body and kissed her pussy through her panties.

"I am surprised that you are wearing panties," Rachel said.

"I like it when someone takes them off me," Mary said.

Rachel slid her panties off and then pushed Mary's legs apart. Mary cupped her tits as she felt Rachel's tongue part her pussy lips. It was a busy tongue that explored everything that it could.

I knew that this woman likes pussy, she thought.

Rachel inserted a couple of fingers into Mary's pussy and worked them hard. Mary enjoyed the double action of being fucked by a couple of fingers and having her clit played with by a soft tongue. It wasn't long before she had a nice little orgasm.

"Thank you," Mary said.

"You are very welcome."

"Let me do you," Mary said.

Rachel stripped and placed her cute little ass above Mary's face. In this position she was able to see and play with Mary's big tits as she got eaten. Mary worked hard and an orgasm came quickly to the little redhead while she squirmed on Mary's face as she hung onto a pair of big tits.

* * * * *

"Now we need a new number four and it will be that guy over there," Mary said to Frank when she got back to their table.

"Mr. Muscles?" Frank said. He was going to ask how the redhead was, but he saved it for later. He knew that he would get all of the details tomorrow. "You want to add him to the list."

"Yeah, he is cute."

Frank groaned. "I'll probably pick him next."

"No, you won't and if you do, I will give you one

do over. Roll."

He nodded. "Thank you."

"But you have a thirty-three percent chance of rolling a guy again." She giggled. "And after that it is another thirty-three percent."

"But isn't there a rule that you can't roll the same number twice, right?"

Mary looked at Frank. "Sure. So that means you now have only a seventeen percent chance of rolling a guy."

"It beats thirty-three." Frank rolled a two. "Yes," a woman.

Mary also rolled a two. They looked at each other and said in unison, "A three-way."

"This will be fun," Mary said.

"Hopefully." Frank looked around and didn't see the little blonde that was number two.

"Let's dance," Mary said.

They found a spot on the dance floor and it wasn't long before another couple tried to dance with them. They weren't up to their standards so this was an unwelcomed advance. Mary was polite but didn't give them any signs to go further.

"What happens if we can't find her?" Frank asked Mary after the couple got the message.

"Then we roll again. Hang on. I will be back shortly." Mary left to go to the toilet.

Frank was surprised, but then noticed that the little blonde was on her way to the toilet as well. He knew that his wife had spotted her and had a plan.

Ten minutes later Mary and the cute little blonde came back from the toilet and appeared to be in deep discussion. It all made sense to Frank now. Mary had made sure that she had bumped into the little blonde. She found out that Cynthia was here with another couple, but were probably open to having her join in.

"How about my husband?" Mary asked her.

"Oh, I don't know. Let me introduce you both to Tracey and Rick and we will see what happens."

The other couple was not bad looking. The woman was a touch overweight, but was still attractive. He was geeky, but in a good way. He was tall and thin, something that Mary liked in a man.

"Would you two like to come back to our hotel room?" Tracey asked Mary. "Cynthia is coming and she is a lot of fun."

Mary didn't have to ask Frank. "We would love to."

Inside the hotel room Cynthia called the other two women to her. She put her arms around them and they formed a circle. "Let's have an all-girl make-out," she said.

Rick came behind Cynthia and undid the back of her dress as she kissed Mary. He pushed the straps off her shoulders and Cynthia allowed the dress to fall to the floor.

"Oh," Frank said when he saw that Cynthia wasn't wearing anything underneath the dress.

Rick moved behind Mary who was now kissing Tracey and started to help Mary out of her clothes.

This guy is a pervert, Frank thought.

He moved behind Cynthia and put his hands on her hips.

"Hi," she said after she spun around. She looked at Frank liked she wanted to be kiss and he took advantage of the opportunity.

Seeing her husband with another woman, Mary spun and kissed Rick. Tracey reached behind Frank and undid his pants. She pulled them to the floor and then reached up and cupped his erection through his underwear. He was hard and she decided to free it.

Cynthia dropped to her knees and Frank watched two women attack his cock with their mouths. He rolled his head back and said, "Oh yeah."

Meanwhile Mary had Rick's head between her giant melons. He was going nuts and pushed the tits into his face. He rubbed his face against them and then sucked one nipple and then the other nipple.

"Do you like them?" Mary asked, purposely sounding surprised even though she wasn't. She knew the effect that her perfect tits had on anyone with a sex drive.

She looked to see what her husband was up to. Frank had the little blonde on the bed and was between her legs. He slid into her and groaned out loud, "Oh my god are you tight."

Cynthia moaned as she took stroke after stroke from Frank's big cock. He was bigger than average and she was smaller than average so that made things a tight fit.

Mary went to the bed and told Tracey to eat her. Then she motioned to Rick to bring his dick over to her so she could suck it. Both of them obeyed her and enjoyed sucking on Rick's cock. It was average size, which was a pleasant change to sucking on Frank's monster. Sometimes her mouth hurt after sucking on Frank.

Mary figured correctly that Tracey was used to eating Cynthia so she knew what to do. "That's nice," Mary purred as she petted the top of the woman's head with her left hand. Her right hand had a cock in it.

"Turnover," Frank said. "Doggie."

The little blonde obeyed and Frank was presented with a tiny ass. "Beautiful," he said as he admired it. He slid into her and she squirmed. Both of them moaned. It was a mutually gratifying fit. Each stroke was pleasure filled and climax wasn't too far off for Frank.

Meanwhile Mary came and Rick was between her legs. Tracey moved over, lifted Cynthia's head and gently rested it on her thighs. "Poor dear," she said while stroking the little blonde's hair. "He is a little big for you." She leaned forward. "Let's speed things up shall we?" She licked her fingers, reached down and flickered Cynthia's clit.

"Oh god," Cynthia shouted over and over again. Between the big dick inside of her and having her clit massaged by someone who knew what they were doing she had no choice but to reach a big climax. She came hard.

"Good," Tracey said. "Me next. Shove your big cock inside of me."

"Okay," Frank said and shoved it in her. It wasn't as tight of a fit, but Frank didn't mind. This was the second woman he had tonight and the third woman he has had today. His dick was happy.

With Cynthia more or less passed out from the onslaught of pleasure, it was now a traditional swap. Both men had the other man's wife in the missionary position. They were side by side on the bed and it was fun.

"I love seeing my wife get nailed by a big cock," Rick said as he watched Tracey squirm with pleasure.

Mary looked at Rick and encouraged him to get off until he did. He came while watching his wife being fucked hard. Mary moved over and did to Tracey what she had done to Cynthia. Mary massaged her clit as Frank's dick worked in and out of her. It didn't take her too long to cum and as she arched her back, Frank decided that it was time for him to fire his load. He did and was the last person to cum.

* * * * *

"Another interesting game," Frank said to Mary on the way home.

Mary rolled her eyes. "Any game where you get your dick wet is an interesting game to you."

"True."

"So, you won the second round. You fucked two women and I only fucked one man. However, I won the first round so I guess that it is a draw."

Frank nodded. He didn't mind that. "So what is the next game?"

"Um...I don't know...yet."

"Will the group be part of it?"

"Yes, I think so."

"Well, whatever game you come up with will be fun."

She smiled.

Part 10:
Blind Dates

Fifteen couples gathered in a two-storey house in the suburbs and represented many facets of the middle class. A few were blue collar, but the majority of them had office jobs. Most were attractive, but not everyone kept their bodies in shape. A few of them were young, a few of them older, but the average person was in their thirties or forties. However, all of them were swingers of various experiences.

Mary and Frank had never been here before and had never met the hosts before. However, there was a chance that they might be back sometime this winter for a swap; who knows how the games will go. Tonight they had been invited by email to join Erin's Swapping Group and as they nursed their drinks Mary wasn't all that comfortable. She was used to being in control and picking who attended her orgies. Even with the last games where she wasn't the Queen of the Orgy it was still her group of swingers so that meant that she was attracted to everyone present. Here, there were a couple of people that she really couldn't see herself being naked with and she knew that Frank felt the same way.

After a half an hour or so of mingling, everyone was asked to gather in the living room for a meeting. Mary and Frank sat in the corner on two chairs. People were in front of them so they couldn't see the person who was speaking very well.

"I am not sure about not knowing who we are going to be hooked up with," Mary said to her husband.

"That's the exciting part of this," Frank whispered to her. It was his idea of answering the email from a friend of a friend of a friend.

She said," If you say so," and stood on the chair so she could see.

A woman spoke to the group of twenty-nine people. She was attractive with curly brown hair and a pleasant figure. "Hello, I'm Erin and welcome to the group. Most of us don't know each other, but soon some of you will get to know each other very well."

This got a few laughs and comments from the group.

"The rules are simple. Each couple draws an envelope that contains three slips of paper and on it are two pieces of information; the person who they are to visit and the date that they are to arrive."

"Only three," someone said.

"For the first round. After that we will see who qualifies for the second round."

"Qualifies?"

"Yes. When a couple visits another couple and nothing happens sexually then both teams have a stroke against them and are at risk to be disqualified for the second round. A couple must have sex with at least two of the three couples to have a chance of qualifying. If they have sex three out of three times then they are guaranteed for the next round."

"What is the second round?"

"You will see."

"What qualifies as sex?"

"Naked with at least a soft swap. By the way, hard swaps are mandatory in the second round so if you are not comfortable with them then don't bother worrying about qualifying."

To Mary soft swaps were: what is the point? Go hard or don't bother.

She looked at Frank and mouthed the words, "Why not?"

Another voice in the crowd asked, "How do you know if couples don't have sex?"

"The honour system, but it will be pretty obvious to us if people are lying."

"How will you know?"

"Oh, we will know." She giggled and clapped her hands. "Right. Come and get your envelopes. One per couple."

Frank came back with a letter sized envelope. Even though nobody was allowed to look at it here, he quietly opened the envelope. Inside were three slips of paper that read:

January 23rd: Jim and Tracey

January 30th: Carl and Lea

February 6th: your place where an unknown couple will visit you

Mary read over his shoulder. "Who are these people?" She whispered in his ears as she looked around.

"Okay, I must break up this party before people figure out who they have gotten. You will start to find out this coming Saturday. Have fun. Be safe."

* * * * *

Mary was nervous as they drove to Jim and Tracey's house. They had no idea who they were and Mary was worried that they were either old or fat, or worse: both.

"We need a signal," Mary said. "In case it is a no-go."

"No, we don't. I will be able to tell if you are into it or not. You set the pace and I will follow."

She groaned. "What if they are fat and ugly?"

"No one says that we have to do anything."

"But we could get disqualified if we don't per-form."

Frank laughed. "No matter what the game is, you have to win it, don't you?"

Mary ignored Frank's obvious statement. "Oh lord

let them be hot."

"Amen sister. Let them be hot so we can fuck them."

"Or at least attractive."

"Why are fat chicks like a riding a moped?"

"Don't know?"

"They are fun to ride until your friends find out."

"Frank!" Mary shook her head. "That was terrible."

He laughed. "Yep, it was."

They pulled into the driveway of a small bungalow that had its front light on. They were expecting company.

"Oh boy, we are supposed to fuck complete strangers."

"Mary that is what we have been doing for years."

"But we have selected them based on looks. This time we have nothing to go on."

"It is a real gamble."

Frank rang the doorbell and Mary chanted in her

head, not fat, not old, not fat, not old, not fat...

Jim smiled as he opened the door and Mary forced a smile. He wasn't exactly fat, but Mary wasn't really attracted to him. She never really liked men who weren't in good shape and he looked like he was only a couple of sessions at the local buffet from becoming fat.

At least he has his hair and isn't ugly, she thought.

"Come in," Jim said. He held the door open for them. "Tracey will be right down. I'll take your coats."

They sat on chair in the living room and Jim left to get the wine.

Frank looked at his wife and she rolled her eyes. He nodded knowingly. "Maybe you can take one for the team?"

She glared at him.

They both heard someone coming down the stairs and turned to see a woman walk down. Unlike Jim she looked like she was in pretty good shape. She wore tight jeans and a tight pink sweater that high-lighted her slim but shapely curves.

She has a nice figure, Mary thought.

"Hello, I'm Tracey," she said.

Pretty, Mary thought. I could do her.

Frank got up and exchanged kisses on the cheek with Tracey. Mary did the same.

Mary decided that tonight her main focus was going to be on Tracey. She was going lesbo for the night. She could tell that Frank was very attracted to Tracey, but she wasn't worried about him; he would fuck almost anything.

Jim opened a bottle of Shiraz and poured everyone a glass.

Mary sat beside Tracey on the chesterfield and asked her, "So how long have you two been swinging?"

"Almost ten years now. We started off slow. We only did soft swaps at first, mostly girl on girl. We only started having hard swaps last year. Our first couple was Erin and Mike."

Mary nodded and took another sip of wine. The more she looked at Tracey the more she wanted to kiss her.

"Before you got into the lifestyle, had you ever been with a girl before?"

"No never. But I had thought about it."

Mary smiled. "May I kiss you?"

Tracey was a little surprised by the question, but smiled. "Yes. I would like that."

The ladies embraced and kissed.

"The women aren't wasting any time are they?" Jim said.

"That is my wife," Frank said. "When she likes something she has to touch it."

Mary felt a small hand on her left tit and did the same favor to Tracey.

"You have really big tits," Tracey said. "Can I see them?"

"Sure." Mary slid the strap off her right shoulder and then did the same for the left. With no support her little black dress fell down to her waist exposing her tits. She wasn't wearing a bra.

"Holy shit," Jim said.

Tracey leaned down and took a nipple into her mouth. Mary leaned back and enjoyed the attention. She was surprised that she felt another pair of lips on her other nipple. She didn't have to open her eyes to see that it was Jim sucking on her tit.

Fine, she thought.

A hand tried to work its way between her legs. Mary spread for it. "Allow me."

Jim's hand massaged Mary's inner thing. Her dress was lifted.

"Go down on me," Mary said to Jim. Then she raised Tracey's chin to look at her. "You are very pretty."

Tracey kissed a pair of Mary's lips as Jim kissed the other pair between her legs. Frank came behind Tracey and admired her shapely ass. She reached down and undid her jeans. Frank pulled them down to reveal a pair of pink panties.

"Very nice," Frank said.

He pulled them off and then his tongue inserted itself between her lips. She moaned, liking what he was doing.

He isn't too bad, Mary thought as she enjoyed what Jim's tongue was doing.

"Sixty-nine," Mary said to Tracey.

Mary lay on the bottom and Tracey lay backwards on top of her. Mary felt a cock enter her as she saw Frank's cock enter Tracey's pussy above her. Mary was happy that she found a way of fucking a man she wasn't attracted to. Thankfully she was attracted to his wife.

She closed her eyes and enjoyed the feeling of Jim's cock going in and out of her as she watched Frank's cock do the same to Tracey. It felt good and this allowed herself to enjoy the experience. He played with her tits and was getting off on them.

"So god damn big," Jim said. "Can I cum on them so my wife can lick it up?"

"Sure," Mary said.

Jim pulled off the condom and fired his load at Mary's tits. He couldn't miss. His entire load landed somewhere on her chest. One shot covered a nipple.

Without a word of protest, Tracey cleaned the cum off Mary's tits. She started cleaning the nipple with

Jim's load on it.

"Very hot," Frank said. He humped harder and was close to cumming.

"Mmm...tastes so good," Tracey said.

Frank groaned loudly and fired his load into the condom that was inside of Tracey.

Mary giggled and glad that it was over. Now all we have to do is fuck one out of the next two couples, she thought. Now to get dress, finish the wine, talk a little and then go home for a good fuck if Frank is up for it. She laughed. Like he isn't horny as hell after being with another couple. He will rock me hard later.

* * * * *

The next Saturday, Mary and Frank were at another strangers' door. This time it was the opposite of the last couple. Mary was attracted to Carl, but not to Lea. As they sat on the chesterfield drinking wine Lea asked Mary if she was bisexual.

"Not really. I'm more bi-friendly," Mary said.

Frank knew exactly why she said that. Lea was a little fat, but what made her unappealing was how plain she looked. She looked like she never heard of make-up or modern hairstyles. It surprised both of them that Carl was a lean mean handsome machine. What was he doing with a dumpy looking woman like Lea?

"I'm not really into women either," Lea said.

"Good. We will concentrate on the men then."

Mary was reminded of the saying that there are no ugly women, just lazy ones. From that point on she only really looked at Carl and he quickly got the message that she was open for business. Carl wasted no time in kissing Mary.

"Oh," Lea said. "My husband is kissing your wife."

"Yes, I can see that," Frank said.

"We should join in."

"Yes we should."

Mary really enjoyed having Carl between her legs and ran her hands over his tight body as he fucked her. He was built and rode her well.

Good steady pace, she thought. Nice cock too. Good size. Hard. Fully erect.

She looked over and saw that Frank was watching her as he fucked Lea. Normally he didn't pay that much attention to her, but she understood why. He needed to look at anywhere but at her.

Good boy, she thought. Take one for the team.

She smiled at him as she enjoyed the pounding that she was receiving. Unlike Frank, she never wanted this to end.

* * * * *

"Two for two," Mary said in the car.

"I just took one for the team," Frank said. He didn't sound happy.

"That you did."

"Now we host."

"Well, we can afford to not do one."

"It will be harder in our home because we can't leave and if we get someone who doesn't get the message then we're screwed."

"Too bad that we couldn't pick and choose from the first two couples."

"Yes, Carl and Tracey. They would make a very cute couple."

* * * * *

Mary decided that she would dress in layers. She would greet the unknown couple in something conservative on top with something slutty underneath. If she liked them then she would quickly peel off the conservative layer.

Dressed in a loosed flowered colored dress that almost went down to her knees she answered the door. Underneath were a pair of hot pants and a tube top that barely covered her boobs. She opened the door and knew that it was only a question of when she was going to drop her dress. Gerri was very similar in appearance to Mary. She was busty and pretty. The only difference was that she was a natural blonde and that Gerri wore a sexy outfit. She was in tight black pants and a low-cut blouse. Mary could see the outline of her pussy lips.

Brad was tall and handsome.

Mary was wet even before the new couple made it to the living room. They sat on the chesterfield and Frank brought out a bottle of wine and glasses. He poured.

"How has your meetings gone so far?" Mary asked.

Brad and Gerri looked at each other. "Well, not great," Gerri said.

Brad added, "We only did it with one couple and it wasn't great. So it is do or die for us."

"You didn't like one of the couples?" Mary asked. "I can understand. We weren't crazy about the two couples that we were with either."

Again, Gerri and Brad exchanged looks, which confused Mary. She burst out laughing and asked, "You mean they didn't like you two?"

Brad nodded.

"What the fuck?" Frank half shouted. "Sorry," he added in a calmer voice.

"You are kidding, right?" Mary asked.

"Why do you say that?" Gerri asked. "Attraction is relative. Not everyone is going to want to get it on with you. A person can't be everyone's type."

Mary shook her head. "Take a good look in the mirror girlfriend. You are everyone's type."

"Hell yes." Frank raised his glass. "Here is to the hottest couple that we've met in Erin's Swapping Group...um, is that what it is called?"

"I think so," Brad answered.

They toasted and drank. Brad returned the toast by also stating that they were the hottest couple that they had met so far.

"Oh, one more thing," Mary said. She stood up, unzipped her dress and let it fall to the floor. "Goodbye conservative look."

"Oh my god," Brad said. He licked his lips as she checked out her hot pants and cleavage. "Awesome."

Gerri reached over and rubbed his crotch. "Good work. You have made my husband hard."

Brad nodded and smiled.

"And you?" Frank asked Gerri.

"I've been wet since we first sat down." She squinted at Frank.

"Here is to fucking," Mary said.

Gerri and Brad exchanged glances and then nodded. Gerri said, "Here is to hot sex with beautiful people."

"Amen to that!" Frank said.

Mary got up and walked over to Brad. Then she straddled him. "Hi," she said. She rubbed her crotch against him and felt his hardness. She felt three hands on her body. She looked over and saw that Gerri was squeezing her right tit. Her pants were unbuttoned and her top came off. Brad and Gerri took a tit each and sucked. Mary leaned back with her eyes closed. "God I love swinging," she said. "Somebody fuck me."

Brad rose to his feet with Mary wrapped around him. "Which way to the bedroom?"

Mary leaned back as far as she could and pointed over her head. "That way," she said.

"Which way," he said. "Sorry, I was looking at your tits."

"Go straight down the hall."

Mary was gently placed on the bed and her pants and panties were pulled off. He stripped and his erection was covered by a condom.

"Easy, big boy," she said. "Go down on me first."

"Yes boss."

She spread for him and he said, "Hello paradise."

Mary barely noticed that the other two had joined them on the bed. Brad's tongue was the only thing that mattered in her world at the moment so she didn't noticed that Frank was doing the same to Gerri.

Mary smiled and welcomed the great orgasm that was on its way. God damn do I love swinging, she thought. Oh, here it comes...

She arched her back and had the best orgasm that she has had in a long time. She came hard and long and then came again. A third orgasm was waiting. Brad replaced his tongue with his cock and filled her up. "Take that beautiful," he said.

She looked up into his eyes and said, "Anytime. Anywhere handsome." Her eyes roamed down his body and was just about to compliment him on his body when the third orgasm caught her by surprise. She screamed out with pleasure and her love juices covered the condom.

Gerri's lips kissed Mary's lips. The two large

breasted pretty women made out as the men humped them. Mary reached under Gerri and played with her clit. Gerri came quickly.

Mary wished that this could last forever and the others also had the same wish.

Now, both Frank and Brad had only one thing to do and it was a difficult task. They had to prolong their erections for as long as possible. With two beautiful women who had gone wild and were really getting off, this was an impossible mission.

The next orgasm that either one of them have I'm done, Frank thought.

As soon as he thought that, Gerri bucked and screamed as she came again. That did it. Both Frank and Brad lost their loads inside of a beautiful woman that was someone else's wife.

* * * * *

As she recovered, Mary couldn't wait for round two, and wasn't only thinking of Erin's games. She wanted these two again.

We've finally met our perfect couple, she thought.

She smiled and felt herself starting to get horny

again.

"What are you thinking?" Frank asked.

"To do it all again," Mary said. "And again and again."

About the Author

Rachel Richards is an oversexed redhead who loves adult playtime and spends her time writing and doing "research" for her erotic novels. Her novels are:

`*Swinger Sex Games'*: a couple invents ways of seducing other couples.

`*She's In Control'*: Prelude to Into the Swing. This is the story of how Kelly and Daniel got together.

`*Into the Swing'*: after a number of false starts, Kelly and Daniel enter into the swinging lifestyle.

`*Full Swing'*: Kelly and Daniel go deeper into the lifestyle and attend their first orgy.

`*50 Shades of Gay'*: an older woman seduces a beautiful young woman into the lesbian world.

`*More 50 Shades of Gay'*: a young beautiful woman experiments with both men and women to determine which sex she prefers.

`*The Promiscuous Games'*: a parody of the Hunger Games where people compete to see who can out sex the other. Only the winner can continue having sex.

`Confessions of a Gym Teacher': Beth Porter is a gym teacher who is tricked into sleeping with some of her older students. Note: all characters are over 18 years of age.

All titles are available as eBooks by Blue Ops on Kindle. The following are Blue Ops Titles by Rachel that are available in paperback:

Kelly's Wild Side

Into the Swing

A Swinging Couple

Swinger Sex Games

www.ingramcontent.com/pod-product-compliance
Lightning Source LLC
Chambersburg PA
CBHW070015260626
47159CB00005B/1811